ELITE SERIES

EDITOR: MARTIN WINDROW

US Army Special Forces 1952-84

Text by GORDON L. ROTTMAN

Colour plates by RON VOLSTAD

OSPREY PUBLISHING LONDON

Published in 1985 by
Osprey Publishing Ltd
Member company of the George Philip Group
12–14 Long Acre, London WC2E 9LP
© Copyright 1985 Osprey Publishing Ltd

Reprinted 1985 (twice), 1986 (twice), 1987, 1988

British Library Cataloguing in Publication Data

Rottman, Gordon L.
    The US Army Special Forces 1952–84.—(Elite; 4)
    1. United States. *Army. Special Forces*—History
    I. Title   II. Series
    356′.167′0973   UA34.S64

    ISBN 0-85045-610-X

Filmset in Great Britain
Printed in Hong Kong through Bookbuilders Ltd

Acknowledgements

This book would not have been possible without the
aid of many others. The author wishes to express his
gratitude to some of many individuals and institutions
for their assistance: Lt. Gen. William P. Yarborough,
USA (Ret.); Col. Aaron Bank, USA (Ret.); Col.
Charles A. Beckwith, USA (Ret.); Col. Cecil B.
Smyth, USA (Ret.); 1st Special Operations
Command (Abn.) Public Affairs Office, especially
Beverly Lindsey; Roxanne Merritt, Curator, Special
Warfare Museum; Shelby Stanton, for sharing his
wealth of knowledge and advice; the Adjutant
General Department of the Louisiana and West
Virginia Army National Guards; the many current
and former Special Forces NCOs who shared their
knowledge; and last but not least my wife, Enriqueta,
for her never-ending support and patience.

Artist's Note

Readers may care to note that the original paintings
from which the colour plates in this book were
prepared are available for private sale. All
reproduction copyright whatsoever is retained by the
publisher. All enquiries should be addressed to:
    Ronald B. Volstad
    PO Box 1577
    Main Post Office
    Edmonton, Alberta
    Canada   T5J 2N9

The publishers regret that they can enter into no
correspondence upon this matter.

Introduction

From its very inception the United States Army Special Forces (SF) has been enmeshed in controversy, its mission misunderstood to varying degrees, and its very existence sometimes opposed by some of the Army hierarchy. Secrecy is an integral part of SF, and the typical SF trooper is one who generally keeps to himself by nature: for these reasons little has been written apart from personal experiences and fiction.

It is only recently that a brief history of SF has been published: *Inside the Green Berets* by Charles M. Simpson III (Col., US Army, Ret.). Only two books of any worth are available on SF's activities in Vietnam: *Vietnam Order of Battle* by Shelby L. Stanton (Capt., US Army, Ret.) and *US Army Special Forces 1961–1971* by Col. Francis J. Kelly. Little else of this organisation's considerable history has been recorded.

The Predecessors

Special Forces traces its family tree to several organisations which evolved during World War II. Here it splits into two branches. Its military branch includes the 1st Special Service Force and the Ranger Infantry Battalions, while its mission and methods of operation are inherited from the Office of Strategic Services.

In June 1942 the US Army activated the first of its Ranger Battalions in Northern Ireland. The Rangers were modelled on the British Commandos and tasked with the same type of mission: i.e. amphibious raids, and seizure of objectives behind enemy lines. The 1st Ranger Bn. took part in the invasion of North Africa, where the 3rd and 4th Bns. were formed. The three battalions then fought in Sicily and Italy, where they were destroyed and disbanded. In the meantime the 2nd and 5th Ranger Bns. were activated in the USA, and subsequently fought in North-West Europe. The

Members of the 77th SFGA undertaking survival training at Camp Hale, Colorado during Exercise 'Lodestar', October 1955. The still-illegal green beret and the World War II Airborne Command patch, as a 'cover', are being worn. (US Army)

6th Ranger Bn. was activated in the Pacific, and operated throughout that theatre.

The 1st Special Service Force (1SSF) was activated on 20 July 1942 at Ft William Henry Harrison, Montana as a special operations force made up of both US and Canadian Army volunteers. It was originally intended for use in a large sabotage/raid operation to be conducted in Norway, Rumania, and Italy, Operation 'Plough', which was subsequently cancelled. The brigade-size unit was highly trained in infantry tactics, sabotage and raid techniques, winter warfare, and amphibious, mountain, ski and parachuting operations. With the cancellation of Operation 'Plough' it was decided to employ the Force in other mountainous, cold-climate areas. The 1SSF subsequently conducted amphibious operations in the Aleutian Islands in 1943, and later in Italy, where it also fought in extensive mountain operations. Additional amphibious assaults were conducted on the southern French coast in 1944. The Force was inactivated in December 1944.

The need for Ranger units was once again

A member of the 77th SFGA searches an 'aggressor', 1955. Both men wear the 'herringbone' fatigues. (US Army)

realised at the beginning of the Korean War in 1950. A total of 14 Ranger Infantry Companies (Airborne) were activated between 1950 and 1951 at Ft Benning, Georgia. The 1st to 5th and 8th Ranger Cos. were moved to Korea and attached to infantry divisions; the other companies were stationed in the USA and West Germany. Due to high casualty rates; to some examples of misuse; to the parallel existence of the 8240th and 8242nd Army Units (classified units with raid and reconnaissance missions); and to the decision to allocate the Ranger Company manning slots to the planned Special Forces, all Ranger Companies were inactivated in 1951.

When the 10th Special Forces Group (Airborne)—(SFGA)—was activated in 1952, it had no lineage of former units to carry on. It was a new organisation with no heritage or traditions. The same applied to the 77th SFGA, activated in 1953, and the 1st SFGA in 1957. An official lineage was retrospectively provided in 1960, with some-what confusing results.

The lineages of the six World War II Ranger Infantry Battalions (including those of the 14 Korean War Ranger Infantry Companies) *and* the 1st Special Service Force were consolidated on 15 April 1960 as the 1st Special Forces, and assigned to the Regular Army. The 1st Special Forces became the parent organisation for all US Army SF units. The 1st Special Forces has no headquarters as it is not a unit as such, but rather a parent organisation

for lineage and historical purposes. The con-solidation of the 1st Special Service Force and the Ranger Battalions was accomplished on paper. The lineage of each battalion headquarters and 'line' company of the 1SSF was combined with that of either a headquarters or a 'line' company of the six Ranger battalions. Additionally some of the 'line' companies of the 1st to 4th Ranger Bns. carried the lineages of the 14 Korean War Ranger Companies. Each of these 'pairings' of unit lineages was assigned to the Headquarters and Headquarters Companies of the 1st to 24th SFGAs. At the time there were only three active SFGAs; on 14 December 1960 four of the SFGAs' lineages were assigned to the Army National Guard and nine to the Army Reserve, while 11 were to remain assigned to the Regular Army. Only seven Regular and seven Reserve SFGAs have ever been formed, however, though all four National Guard SFGAs have been formed at one time or another.

This rather tortuous process now gave SF a lineage, a heritage. The lineage carried credits in two wars, several theatres of operation, numerous campaigns, and even amphibious and airborne assaults. In the long run it was to create some problems, however. At that time the Army had no plans to activate Ranger units in the future. History provided no other examples of US Army units which had foreshadowed SF's guerrilla warfare mission. The assignment of the 1st Special Service Force's and the Rangers' lineage seemed appro-priate at the time.

All SFGA designations are officially followed by '1st Special Forces' to signify this lineage; e.g. '8th SFGA, 1st SF'. Other SF units, such as separate companies and detachments, also carry the 1st SF designation, but they are new units not carrying the lineage of specific 1SSF and Ranger units as the SFGA headquarters do.

Current and Vietnam era US Army Ranger units carry the lineage of the 75th Infantry, which is loosely connected to the 5307th Composite Unit (Provisional), better known as 'Merrill's Ma-rauders'. The question of whether or not to separate the SF and Ranger lineages once again is currently under study.

There is another lineage to which, in the opinion of some, the SF has a claim. The Office of Strategic Services (OSS) was formed in 1941 as the US

A captain of the 1st SFGA involved in Exercise 'Long Pass', Clark Air Force Base, Philippines, February 1961. He wears the olive green (OG) 107 fatigues with a personally added sleeve pocket. The crudely embroidered infantry crossed rifles were probably made on Okinawa. (US Army)

parachuted into occupied countries to contact resistance groups. They provided liaison with Allied headquarters, arranged for equipment and supply airdrops, trained the resistance in the use of weapons, and co-ordinated attacks on German forces.

There were certain other OSS operations which bore a more striking resemblance to future SF missions. One was Detachment 101, which operated in Burma organising thousands of local tribesmen into the 'Kachin Rangers', and wreaked havoc behind Japanese lines. Another was Detachment 202, which conducted strategic reconnaissance missions behind Japanese lines in China.

After World War II the lineage of the OSS's Special Intelligence and part of the Special Operations Branches were assigned to the new Central Intelligence Agency. Certainly, some of the organisations within OSS should have been used to draw the SF lineage, since they were much more operationally compatible with the SF mission than were the 1st Special Service Force and the Rangers.

The Beginnings

counterpart of the British Special Operations Executive (SOE). Its activities varied greatly, and involved many special operations and guerrilla warfare missions.

The Operational Groups (OG) had the mission of providing operational nucleii for guerrilla organisations which had been formed from resistance groups in enemy-occupied territory. The 34-man OGs organised and trained these groups in techniques of resistance, provided them with supplies, and co-ordinated their activities with Allied plans. They also conducted independent raids on targets deep in enemy-held territory. Strategic intelligence collection was another mission performed by the OG, which infiltrated enemy territory by land, sea, or air. Most of these operations were conducted in France, Italy, Greece, Yugoslavia, and South-East Asia.

The Special Operations Branch's 'Jedburgh' Teams had a different mission. They consisted of two officers and an enlisted radio operator, and were made up of American, British, French, Dutch, and Belgian personnel. Over 80 teams were

The world was in an unsettled condition in the early 1950s. The Korean War had broken out; there were dozens of Communist-inspired and -backed rebellions and civil wars in progress; and massive Soviet forces were poised on the borders of Western Europe. It was in this setting that the seed for Special Forces was germinated. The seed had been planted by Brig. Gen. Robert A. McClure, Chief of the Army Psychological Warfare Staff Section; and the unlikely garden plot was in the forest of the Pentagon.

Gen. McClure's goal was to form a guerrilla or unconventional warfare (UW) organisation within the US Army: a difficult task, as the Army was conventional in thought, convinced that 'push button' warfare was well within sight, felt it could rely on nuclear weapons, and tended to regard so-called 'élite' units with some disdain.

To accomplish his goal Gen. McClure formed a Special Operations Section under his staff in 1951. Heading it was Col. Wendell Fertig, while the Plans Officer was Col. Russell W. Volckman. Both had commanded guerrillas in the Philippines. The

Members of the West Virginia Army National Guard's 16th SFGA during their annual training at Ft Bragg, July 1960. As the beret was still unauthorised, they wear the regulation 'Ridgeway' field cap. Two types of outdated rank insignia are being worn. (US Army)

Operations Officer was Col. Aaron Bank, a former Jedburgh Team member with three missions into France and one into Indochina under his belt. The section also included other former members of OSS, Merrill's Marauders, and other World War II special operations organisations.

These pioneers in modern UW doctrine developed operational concepts, individual and unit training programmes, proposals for wartime contingency plans, tables of organisation and equipment for proposed units, and countless staff briefings to sell their theories to the Army hierarchy. Besides bringing to this task their vast personal experiences, they based many of their concepts on the OSS's Special Operations Branch (the Jedburghs) and Operational Group Command. Training, organisation, and techniques of operations were derived from those programmes.

The tradition-bound Army produced many opponents of the concept of a formally organised unit with the mission of guerrilla warfare. Outside of the OSS—considered an unusual organisation at best—there had been nothing like it before. It meant providing manpower slots at the cost of 'real' combat units, and it might mean that another 'élite'

formation would appear. Guerrilla warfare and other special operations were looked upon by many as a minor effort that could not have a major impact on the overall outcome of a war. Special operations units were also condemned for drawing off valuable and skilled manpower needed elsewhere. (This argument has force; but opponents fail to see the value of the possible rewards from the results achieved by special operations units if supported and properly employed.) The stumbling blocks were many; and not all were produced by the Army.

The new CIA (backed quietly by the State Department) and the US Air Force were also major opponents. They had jointly developed their own plans for the conduct of UW in any future war. The Air Force envisioned the use of massive airpower to bring an enemy to its knees. CIA agents were to be dropped into enemy territory to organise guerrillas. They were to be supplied by airdrop provided by the Air Force, and were to receive tactical close air support. The guerrillas, under CIA control and supported by the Air Force, were to further disrupt the enemy forces disorganised by Air Force bombs in their rear areas, while the Army merely mopped up after the devastation caused by the Air Force in the front lines.

The Army and Air Force/CIA proposals were brought before the Joint Chiefs of Staff in early 1952. The Air Force contended that guerrilla operations would be conducted in strategic areas, which were their turf. Likewise the CIA maintained that it was responsible for behind-the-lines covert activities. The CIA lost out when it was decided that the Department of Defense would be responsible for organising guerrilla forces within war zones. As the Army was responsible for ground combat, it was charged with organising these forces, while the Air Force was tasked to support them.

The Army in the meantime reluctantly accepted the proposals for a UW organisation. Gen. J. Lawton Collins, Army Chief of Staff, backed the idea, and was able to sell it to President Eisenhower; 2,300 manning slots were made available, primarily by the decision to inactivate the 14 Ranger Companies. (The theory seemed to be that special operations units all have the same function and could perform each other's rôles with little difficulty—a consensus of misunderstanding that still persists today, although to a lesser degree.) The title for this new organisation was Special Forces, originally a 1944 term used to identify collectively all OSS and British SOE operating units. The group organisation was borrowed from that of the OSS Operational Group Command, but expanded to make it more self-sufficient.

In April 1952 Col. Aaron Bank was reassigned to the Psychological Operations Division (then at Ft Riley, Kansas, and a component of the General Staff School) and sent to Ft Bragg, North Carolina with instructions to select a site for the future Psychological Warfare School and the planned SF unit. On 20 June 1952 the 10th Special Forces Group (Airborne) was activated at Ft Bragg under the command of Col. Bank. It was activated without fanfare or publicity. The group was quartered in World War II barracks in a section of the post known as Smoke Bomb Hill—a name that became part of the SF vocabulary.

Recruiting had begun in April, when a pamphlet was distributed outlining the requirements to be met in order to volunteer for the new organisation. It was worded to appeal to the kind of men that Bank was looking for: skilled professionals, mature individuals willing to accept responsibilities beyond their rank, those experienced in travel overseas and skilled in a foreign language, and willing to take risks not expected of conventional units. The volunteers began to appear in May, and were just what Bank was looking for—Paratroopers and Rangers; former OSS personnel; former members of Merrill's Marauders, 1st Special Service Force, Ranger battalions, and every other World War II special operations unit that had existed, including Lodge Act personnel (displaced persons from Communist-dominated countries who would receive US citizenship in exchange for a hitch in the Army). There were also some younger, less experienced soldiers, but all professionals regardless.

Former OSS and other experienced officers were quickly formed into a training staff to develop the unit's training programme. Training began at the individual level, and all troops were trained in their respective speciality: operations and intelligence, weapons, demolitions, communications, and medical. Speciality cross-training was also begun. Emphasis was placed on the many aspects of UW to

Three NCOs of the 7th SFGA on a temporary duty tour in Vietnam, 1961. They are outfitted in the spotted camouflage uniform and are armed with German World War II MP.40 submachine guns. (Author's collection)

include security, sabotage, formation and operation of intelligence and escape and evasion systems (called 'nets' by the Army), and so on. Training progressed to team level and cross-training was continued, conducted within and by the teams. Team members had to show initiative, be able to instruct others, and possess leadership and organisational skills. The Psychological Warfare Center and School was established at Ft Bragg in October 1952, with the SF School as a component element.

In October the 10th SFGA began a group-level manoeuvre in Georgia's Chatahoochie National Forest. The planning staff modelled the exercise on those conducted by the Jedburgh Teams; and it was to begin a tradition of SF's use of civilian involvement in its training exercises. Civilians living in the area acted as a guerrilla support organisation, providing live and dead letter drops, safe houses, information on aggressor forces, and operating an escape and evasion net. Local law enforcement agencies and a Georgia Army National Guard military police unit acted as the aggressor counter-guerrilla force. SF teams were rotated in the rôle of guerrillas.

Advanced training in amphibious operations was

followed by mountain and cold weather training in Colorado. The next phase was the conduct of the Army Training Test, a battalion of the 82nd Airborne Division providing the aggressors, which was to become another tradition. The tests were totally successful. Sixty-four members of the 10th SFGA were sent to Korea in early 1953 to act as UW advisors to Far East Command, but no actual detachments were deployed.

It was in June 1953 that the workers' revolt broke out in Communist-dominated East Berlin. It was quickly and harshly crushed, but it had the effect of making the Army realise that 10th SFGA needed to be in Europe in order to respond rapidly to critical situations. About half of the group's assigned strength, 782 troops, sailed to Germany in November. The other half—primarily the new arrivals who were not fully trained, plus a cadre of trained officers and NCOs—remained to form the 77th Special Forces Group (Airborne), which had been activated on 23 September. The 10th was quartered in the luxurious Flint Kaserne in the Bavarian town of Bad Tölz.

Two HALO-trained A Teams don their A/P28S free-fall parachutes at Pope Air Force Base outside Ft Bragg. A C-130 transport waits in the background. (US Army)

The 10th SFGA continued to train in its new surroundings, making use of the local population in its exercises; German border police, US troops, and Allied units made excellent guerrilla and counter-guerrilla forces. The 10th also acted as aggressors for exercises by conventional units when the employment of guerrillas was desired. Training exercises, exchange programmes, and mobile training teams were soon being mounted in other countries.

The 77th SFGA trained up to group level and was prepared for world-wide deployment. The Psychological Warfare Center was redesignated the Special Warfare Center and School on 1 May 1957.

It was in the mid-1950s that SF began to look to the Far East. It was obvious that trouble was brewing in the area. The 77th formed and sent two special training teams to Japan in 1956. They conducted training missions in various South-East Asian countries—including a place called South Vietnam. In 1957 these two teams were moved to Okinawa, and formed the cadre for the 1st Special Forces Group (Airborne) activated on 24 June at Ft Buckner. The 1st began deploying teams to Vietnam, Thailand, and Nationalist China as well as to other Allied countries throughout Asia and the Pacific.

In July 1959 the 77th SFGA deployed Operation 'White Star' to Laos for the purpose of training the Royal Laotian Army. The teams (later augmented by the 1st SFGA) were redesignated White Star Mobile Training Teams in April 1961, and remained there until October 1962. The 77th was redesignated 7th SFGA on 20 May 1960 to place its designation in line with projected groups.

An old enemy in a new form began to rear its ugly head in the late-1950s. Instead of massed tank armies swarming across Western Europe, guerrilla warfare was being used to achieve political/military goals in other parts of the world. SF now became concerned about this aspect of UW—counterinsurgency. They were to be the guerrillas themselves in a sense, but now they were increasingly involved in training small countries' armed forces to combat guerrillas.

Expansion and Growth

President John F. Kennedy's concern over the increase in the number of Communist-inspired 'wars of liberation' had a great influence on the expansion of SF. The logic was simple: what better force to combat guerrillas than one trained as guerrillas themselves? UW was still to remain SF's primary mission, but assisting small nations in their counterinsurgency efforts became a major effort.

In October 1961 President Kennedy visited Ft Bragg to see for himself the capabilities of this little-known organisation. A massive effort had been made by the Special Warfare Center and the 7th SFGA to impress the President. Their demonstrations of techniques and equipment made a favourable impression. Fully realising the turn that world events were taking, the President ordered the expansion of SF.

Expansion of a force that requires high quality personnel and lengthy specialist training brings its own inherent problems, and SF was no exception. The three existing groups were brought up to strength. Funds were made available for much-needed equipment and training. The 5th SFGA was activated on 5 December 1961 to support missions in South-East Asia. The 3rd, 6th, and 8th SFGAs were formed in 1963. To support this massive expansion, the SF Training Group was

The tactical operations centre of the Army Reserve's 24th SFGA on Hawaii, early 1960s. (Author's collection)

formed to provide a continuous flow of personnel.

Small SF units had first been formed in the Army Reserve and Army National Guard in 1959. In 1961 these units were expanded into the 2nd, 9th, 11th, 12th, 13th, 17th, and 24th Reserve and the 16th, 19th, 20th, and 21st National Guard SFGAs. In 1966 these small groups were consolidated into the Reserve's 11th and 12th and the National Guard's 19th and 20th SFGAs.

It must be admitted that this expansion did lower the overall quality of SF personnel. Selection and training standards were relaxed somewhat, although the personnel were still triple volunteers, and of much higher quality than the bulk of the Army. In 1965 first enlistment soldiers and second lieutenants were allowed to volunteer for the first time. To gain public support and sufficient volunteers, publicity campaigns were instituted which caused some displeasure among the old hands, and amusement among SF's detractors.

Though there were problems involved in SF's expansion, there were also benefits. The increased recruiting efforts and publicity attracted many high quality troops who may not have had an opportunity to volunteer in the past. The development of new items of equipment and techniques of operation would not have been possible without the expansion programme. Training funds for both individuals and units, so critical in the development of an effective organisation, would otherwise have been out of reach. Regardless of its growing pains, SF accomplished the multitude of missions assigned to it. From entire groups down to a single individual, detachments were deployed

Brig.Gen. William P. Yarborough, Special Warfare Center Commanding General, and a British SAS officer confer during a guerrilla warfare exercise near Andrews, North Carolina, September 1960. The general wears a modified fatigue shirt from which the later jungle fatigues were derived. (US Army)

on countless missions to just about every Allied and friendly country.

The 1st SFGA continued to deploy teams throughout Asia and the Pacific area. They conducted innumerable civic action projects, trained military and police in counterinsurgency, conducted special operations in South-East Asia (often in support of other SF units already deployed there), and were instrumental in training and developing many nations' own SF units. Laos, Thailand, the Philippines, South Vietnam, South Korea, and Taiwan were the countries in which most of the operations took place.

The 3rd SFGA was activated on 5 December 1963 at Ft Bragg. It was made responsible for Africa, where a number of small and mostly unpublicised missions were conducted in the Cameroons, Congo, Ethiopia, Guinea, Kenya, Mali, Senegal, and other countries. The 10th SFGA had been involved in some of these prior to the formation of the 3rd. Most of these were small scale

advisory and assistance operations, although a team from the 10th accomplished a risky rescue of over 200 Belgian refugees during the 1960 Congo revolution.

For a brief period prior to the activation of the 6th SFGA on 1 May 1963 at Ft Bragg, Company C of the 10th was responsible for North Africa, the Middle East, and part of South-West Asia. The 6th took over responsibility for the Middle East in 1964. Training missions were conducted by SF in Iran, Jordan, Pakistan, Saudi Arabia, Turkey and elsewhere, and SF was instrumental in developing these nations' own special operations units.

Concern over the situation in Latin America due to the proliferation of insurgency movements in a region so close to home led to what would become one of the larger operations outside South-East Asia. The 7th SFGA, as part of its world-wide deployment mission, began conducting advisory operations in various Latin American countries in 1961. Company D of the 7th was moved to the Panama Canal Zone the following year. The next year it was to form the nucleus for the 8th SFGA, activated on 1 April at Ft Gurlick. The 8th sent training teams to almost every country in Central and South America where civic action operations, counterinsurgency training, and development of various special operations units were successfully accomplished.

With all of these missions being conducted throughout the world, the major concern of SF was a remote little corner of Asia that few Americans had even heard of. The first SF unit to operate in South-East Asia was a detachment from the 77th SFGA which trained the Thai Rangers in 1954. The first SF unit in Vietnam was the 14th Special Forces Operational Detachment (SFOD), formed from personnel of the 77th, which spent a brief period there in 1957 training Vietnamese Commandos. Thus began what was to become the largest, longest, and most controversial of SF's many missions.

Vietnam

The first teams of the 1st SFGA arrived in Vietnam in late 1957. There had already been a US presence there since 1950 in the form of the US Military Assistance Advisory Group Indochina.

Vietnam was a country divided. With the defeat of the French Union forces by the Viet Minh (Communist Vietnam Independence League), the former French colony of Indochina (made up of the three semi-autonomous 'countries' of Vietnam, Laos, and Cambodia) were given their independence by agreement to Geneva accords in 1954. Vietnam was divided into a Communist-controlled North Vietnam and a Western-oriented South Vietnam. A brief peace ensued, but it was not long before the Communist National Liberation Front and its military arm, the Viet Cong, made its presence known. They received support from North Vietnam in the form of limited amounts of supplies, weapons, and infiltrated cadre personnel.

Since 1957 SF had been training Vietnamese personnel at the Commando Training Center in Nha Trang. These men would eventually become the nucleus for the Vietnamese SF. Members of the 77th SFGA began training the first Vietnamese Ranger units shortly afterwards. The mission continued with the primary task of providing the Army of the Republic of Vietnam (ARVN) with its own special operations and offensive UW units. Teams from both the 1st and 77th (later 7th) SFGAs were deployed to Vietnam for this purpose. Until 1961 the US advisory effort was oriented towards developing the ARVN into a conventional force capable of defending the new nation from a Korean-style invasion by North Vietnam: a rôle that was to change.

In the early 1960s the Vietnamese government had virtually no military or administrative control over the Central Highlands and large areas of the Mekong Delta. Control of these areas by the government were critical. Just as neglected were the various minority groups which populated them.

The development of indigenous minority groups into a military force has always been a recognised SF concept. Living in remote rural areas, often in poverty, they are used to physical hardship, and they know the area and how to survive in it. Due to their minority status, however, they tend to be somewhat neglected, ignored or even persecuted by the national government. Their situation varies from complacency with their lot to discontent verging on rebellion. Either way, they are generally ripe for exploitation by whichever side reaches them first. This may mean anything from forced service in an insurgent unit to total inclusion in the legal government's national goals. One hazard for the legal government is that even though a minority group may side with it, their ultimate goals may not necessarily be the same. In Vietnam's case the problems were further aggravated by the centuries-old racial and religious prejudices of the ethnic Vietnamese.

Vietnam has a number of ethnic and religious minorities, which were ignored or actually ill-treated by the government in Saigon. The VC were

An A Team of the 7th SFGA providing a demonstration of parachute equipment in the Panama Canal Zone, 1962. The parachute is the T-10. The M1951 mountain rucksack is rigged under the reserve parachute. (US Army)

beginning to exploit these groups. In order to secure the critical areas, expand government presence, limit the exploitation of the minorities, and bring them into the national struggle, it was decided to employ SF elements to organise them into local self-defence forces.

The heart of most SF efforts in Vietnam was the Civilian Irregular Defense Group programme (CIDG—pronounced 'cidge'); it was begun in 1961 as the Area Development Program, and was not officially designated CIDG until the following year. The CIDG were civilian employees of the US Army, and not part of the ARVN. They were recruited, trained, clothed, equipped, fed, housed, and paid by the USSF. The CIDG programme was initially composed exclusively of Montagnards (French for 'highlanders'). The Montagnards, who were of a completely different racial stock than the Vietnamese, had long been despised by them; referred to as *moi* (savages), they were not recognised as citizens. They are simple people who do not have a common language, and in the more remote areas it is difficult for them to understand the dialect of the village on a neighbouring mountain. Only the Jarai and Rhade, the most advanced tribes, had a crude written language. The SF troops quickly developed a close relationship with these simple people, and in many cases were even made members of the tribe in elaborate ceremonies. A dangerous situation did develop in 1964 when some Rhade Montagnard strike forces revolted and killed some Vietnamese SF troops; the

Radio operators of the 5th SFGA operate an AN/GRA-109 radio powered by a G-13 generator, Ft Bragg, 1962. They wear the M1953 field jacket. (US Army)

USSF managed to negotiate a peaceful settlement.

The first experimental SF camp was established at Buon Enao, near Ban Me Thuot, by half of 1st SFGA's Detachment A-35 in late 1961. The purpose of the programme was to establish and train both village defence and local security forces for some 40 villages in the area. It was so successful that by the next year over 200 villages were involved in the programme with 12,000 armed Rhade Montagnards.

During 1962 a number of separate counterinsurgency and paramilitary programmes were instituted by the US Military Assistance Advisory Command Vietnam and the CIA's US Operations Mission. These were all to be incorporated into the CIDG programme under the auspices of SF on 1 July 1963. Besides village security and defence, the CIDG were progressively tasked with more aggressive missions. A Mountain Commando (later Mountain Scouts) Training Center was established, and reconnaissance missions were conducted into remote areas. Another programme was the Trailwatchers (later Border Surveillance), which conducted surveillance missions on infiltration trails in the border areas. The village defence programme was expanded into other areas of Vietnam as well. By the end of 1963 there were 18,000 CIDG strike force and 43,000 hamlet militia (the redesignated village self-defence) troops advised by two B Teams and 22 A Teams.

US Army Special Forces Vietnam (Provisional) or USASFV—in effect, a small SF group—was formed in September 1962 for the control of all SF elements in the country. Teams from the 1st, 5th, and 7th SFGAs were rotated to Vietnam for six-month temporary duty hours. This system had the advantage of retaining team integrity, but it sacrificed continuity of the advisory effort, and forced the relieving team to learn the area, the troops, and the effective methods of operation anew with each rotation. The in-country team provided the relieving team with information on the area and their operations, and upon their arrival conducted briefings and orientation patrols before departing.

By 1964 the CIDG were actively conducting strike operations, and had expanded to include other minority groups. These included the Khmers (ethnic Cambodians born and raised in Vietnam), Nungs (ethnic Chinese mountain tribesmen),

Chams and other ethnic Chinese from the coastal regions, and the Cao Dai and Hoa Hao militant religious sects (ethnic Vietnamese). These minority groups and their SF advisors rapidly developed a mutual respect and loyalty; many of the kind of men that SF attracts have a natural leaning towards the 'underdog' to begin with.

Although highly conducive to the war effort and the accomplishment of assigned unit missions, this close relationship between the CIDG strikers and the SF troopers led to the almost total exclusion of the Vietnamese SF (Lac Luong Dac Biet—LLDB) from the chain of command in many strike forces. The predominantly Vietnamese (and usually prejudiced) LLDB were officially in command of the strike forces, while the USSF were supposedly to act only as advisors to them; this was often not the case in practice.

The Vietnamese SF were formed in 1957 from a group of 58 men trained by the 14th SFOD; these men became the cadre for the Vietnamese 77th Observation Group, an SF-type unit. After several reorganisations it evolved in 1963 into the LLDB Command, similar to a USSF group. An LLDB team (slightly smaller than its USSF counterpart) was assigned to each strike force camp.

Sad to say, the relationship between the USSF team and its LLDB counterpart was not always as it

should have been. Attitudes ranged from totally ignoring each other to outright hostility in a few instances. In most cases, though, a workable relationship evolved, and things ran more or less smoothly. Quite often the LLDB handled the day-to-day administration and operation of the camp, while the USSF ran the combat operations of the strike force. There were a number of reasons for this conflict, and a simple clash of cultures was a primary one. The LLDB were not necessarily as well trained as their US counterparts; but they had been at it for a long time, and would remain at it long after the 'hard charging' Americans had completed their six-month tour and had been replaced by more Americans, with more new ideas on how to change things. There were cases of corruption, laziness, and reluctance to fight on the part of some members of the LLDB, but there were also many good ones. It was not unusual for an LLDB team and its USSF counterpart to develop a good working relationship.

A lesser problem also developed in that conventional US units and higher commanders often looked upon the CIDG as SF's 'private army'.

13

The problem was compounded by the fact that strike companies and combat reconnaissance platoons were in practice commanded by SF NCOs, often junior ones, in positions held by captains and lieutenants in conventional units. More than one battalion commander was surprised to find that the company commander with whom he had been conducting a joint operation was only a buck sergeant.

In September 1964 USASFV was disbanded, and the 5th SFGA was relocated to Vietnam by phasing in its teams. There were now some 40 camps. The six-month tour became a thing of the past, and one-year tours were required, as by other US personnel. This meant that a team was assigned to a specific camp where it remained. The personnel rotated in and out of the teams on their one-year tours, thus ensuring a continuity of the advisory effort, as there were always 'old hands' in the teams who were familiar with the strike force and the area. The arrival of the 5th SFGA also signalled another expansion of the CIDG programme.

The war was escalating at a rapid pace. North Vietnamese Army (NVA) units, and massive amounts of supplies and equipment, were flowing into the south by way of the Ho Chi Minh Trail network through Laos and Cambodia. By 1967 it could no longer be termed a guerrilla war: massive, prolonged multi-division battles were being fought by both sides.

The primary missions of the strike force camps were border security, infiltration trail network interdiction, local village security, civic action and medical coverage for the local populace, and general intelligence collection. In addition SF also had an advisory rôle for the Regional and Popular Forces (RF/PF or 'Ruff-Puffs'—territorial and local militia) in some areas. By 1969 the CIDG had grown into a well-armed and trained professional force, with its own traditions and lineages, of almost 40,000 strikers in the Camp Strike Forces alone. Several thousands more were employed by the Mobile Strike Forces and reconnaissance projects. All were trained, advised, and supported by a mere 2,300 USSF.

The Mobile Strike Force ('Mike Force') concept grew out of a need for SF to have a reaction force under its own control to reinforce camps that were under attack or siege. US and ARVN units could

The Commander of the 7th SFGA observes his men's training at the Northern Warfare Center, Ft Greely, Alaska, October 1963. This is a rare instance of the beret flash being worn on a field cap. (US Army)

not always be relied upon to provide this support when, where, and in the manner needed. The concept was derived from a II Corps reaction force known as 'Eagle Flight', formed in late 1964. Since the early 1960s the term 'mobile strike force' had been used to designate locally raised reaction forces as well. In July 1965 a battalion-size Mobile Strike Force was authorised for each C Team for employment in their corps area. A fifth force was formed for employment by the 5th SFGA on a country-wide basis to provide an additional back-up element. Each had an A Team in command of it, and did not receive an LLDB team until late 1966.

That same year their strength was increased to between two and five battalions each, plus a reconnaissance company. In late 1967 a B Team was assigned to each Mike Force, providing a Mobile Strike Force Command for each corps area (1st to 4th) and the 5th directly under group control. The 1st, 2nd, and 5th were predominantly Montagnards, while the 3rd and 4th were mostly Nungs and Cambodians. They were airborne-qualified at the SF-run jump school at the LLDB Training Center, trained in more offensive-type operations, and more heavily armed than their Camp Strike Force comrades. The Mike Forces took part in a large number of operations which saved or took the pressure off hard-pressed camps. Additionally they conducted their own offensive operations, along with three successful battalion-size airborne assaults in 1967 and one in 1968.

An off-shoot of the Mike Force concept was the Mobile Guerrilla Force created in mid-1966. These consisted of a specially trained CIDG Strike Force Company and a Reconnaissance Platoon under the command of a USSF A Team with no LLDB. One was assigned to each corps area, with the mission to infiltrate remote enemy-controlled areas and conduct ambushes and raids; these 'Blackjack' operations were very effective. At the end of 1967 the MGFs were absorbed into the expanding Mike Forces, which continued similar missions.

The height of SF deployment in Vietnam was 1969. The 5th SFGA was organised and deployed as follows:

The Special Forces Operations Base (SFOB) was at Nha Trang. It contained the Group Headquarters, Signal Company, Logistical Support Center, 5th Mobile Strike Force Command (SFOB B-55), and numerous special detachments (military intelligence, signal, engineer, etc.). The Military Assistance Command Vietnam (MACV) Recondo School (operated by 5th SFGA since 1966) was also here.

Companies C, B, A, and D were responsible for the I, II, III, and IV CTZs respectively.[1] Each had one C Team, two to four B Teams, and from eight to

Two members of the 5th SFGA planning a patrol during Exercise 'Polar Siege', Ft Richerson, Alaska, February 1964. They wear the OG 107 parka with fur-ruffed hood and three-finger arctic mittens. Pinned to their shoulder is the old 'aggressor' insignia, a green triangle. By this time the 5th SFGA had adopted an embroidered flash. (US Army)

14 A Teams. Company E was responsible for special missions, and had eight B Teams.

The C Teams were co-located (except for that of Company E) with an LLDB C Team, and provided command and control and logistical support for its A and B Teams. One B Team in each company was the Mobile Strike Force Command while the others, usually located in province capitals, controlled a varied number of A Teams. There was a counterpart LLDB A and B Team co-located with each USSF one.

A Camp Strike Force consisted of three or four 130-man companies, a Combat Reconnaissance Platoon, and a Political Warfare (civic action) Team. Many camps had an ARVN artillery platoon (two 105 mm howitzers) attached.

The camps were usually established in remote areas where they could conduct border surveillance and interdiction missions, or further back from the border where they were situated to interdict infiltration trail networks. Usually the companies were rotated between week-long combat patrols, camp security, and training. Two USSF and one

---

[1]South Vietnam was divided into four Corps Tactical Zones (CTZ) for regional command and control. These were ARVN commands, but they were used by US forces because of their convenience of designating areas within the country. US forces had their own command structure overlaid on the ARVN CTZs. In 1972 these were redesignated Military Regions.

LLDB normally accompanied each combat operation. They operated in their assigned tactical area of responsibility of perhaps 100 to 200 square kilometres, but this varied greatly depending on the area. Occasionally joint operations were conducted with US or ARVN units.

The camp units were generally very good, but they did have their limitations. Being local paramilitary troops, they would often lose their motivation if deployed away from their home area. Their level of training and loose discipline limited their ability to execute complex, long-range, or long-term operations. They were lightly armed, and fire discipline was sometimes lax and erratic. So long as these limitations were allowed for, the CIDG were well suited for reconnaissance, interdiction, and harassing missions usually conducted in much the same manner as VC operations.

In the early days the camps were constructed of locally available materials and were often weakly defended. Quarters and support buildings were built of scrap lumber, corrugated metal, logs, and thatching. Defences usually included some machine gun bunkers, a few mortar pits, a surrounding trench or berm, punji stakes, a little barbed wire, and sometimes a shallow moat. In the mid-1960s the camps began to be 'hardened' and to be termed 'fighting' camps. More machine guns, mortars, and recoilless rifles were added, perimeter fighting positions were improved, more barbed and concertina wire and claymore mines were emplaced, and an inner perimeter was constructed. The inner perimeter was capable of holding out even if the remainder of the camp was overrun. It contained the USSF and LLDB team houses, communications bunker, supply room, and ammunition bunkers. The outer perimeter area contained CIDG quarters and sometimes quarters for families, if they did not live in a nearby village. Many camps were a self-contained community with tailor and barber shops, medical dispensary, school, and recreational facilities. Most had an airstrip, and all had a helipad. In many rugged mountainous areas, and often in the Mekong Delta, there was no space for an airstrip: many of these camps could only be reached by helicopter or, in the latter case, by boat. The delta region even required floating camps due to almost year-round flooding.

The VC and NVA could and did overrun some camps, so long as they were willing to pay the price. It was more of a propaganda/political victory than

A captain of the 6th SFGA presents a pre-jump briefing to Reservists of 17th SFGA during Exercise 'Tanana Flats II', Ft Wainwright, Alaska, July 1965. The three Regular Army captains wear the early version tropical fatigues. The captain with the beret wears Vietnamese SF jumpwings below his name tape and the Vietnamese ranger badge above it. The Reservists wear the OG 107 fatigues. The young sergeant has illegally cut down his fatigues to make a short-sleeve shirt. (US Army)

a military one. Other camps came close to being overrun, and still others suffered lengthy sieges. VC infiltrated into the strike force were responsible for the fall of some camps.

The 5th SFGA also conducted a large number of special operations in Vietnam, under the control of Company E; long-range reconnaissance and intelligence collection were normally the goal. The 'Greek-letter' projects conducted most of these operations. The first, Project Delta (SFOD B-52), was formed in 1964. Projects Omega (SFOD B-50) and Sigma (SFOD B-56) were formed in 1966. They consisted of reconnaissance teams, 'roadrunner' teams (CIDG disguised as VC/NVA), and a reaction force unit. Other intelligence collection activities were conducted by SFODs B-53 and B-57 (Project Gamma). Besides operating in Vietnam, some missions were infiltrated into neighbouring countries. SFOD B-51 operated the LLDB Training Center, which also provided courses for the CIDG.

Military Assistance Command Vietnam, Studies and Observation Group (MACV-SOG)—often referred to as the Special Operations Group—was formed in January 1964 as a joint service unconventional warfare task force. It was initially headquartered in Cholon and moved to Saigon in 1966. Most of the Army personnel were SF and assigned on paper to Special Operations Augmentation (SOA), 5th SFGA as a cover. It was not part of the 5th SFGA and was not actually an SF unit. Its mission was to advise and support the Vietnamese Special Exploitation Service (later the Strategic Technical Directorate). Its ground reconnaissance elements were organised into Command and Control North, Central, and South (CCN, CCC, CCS). They conducted reconnaissance and direct action missions into North Vietnam, Laos, and Cambodia. Each 'CC' was made up of Spike reconnaissance teams, Hatchet strike platoons, and SLAM exploitation companies.

The withdrawal of US forces from Vietnam began in 1970. SF began to phase out its programme by transferring most to the ARVN. The camps were either converted to RF/PF units or into a new organisation under the ARVN Ranger Command, the Border Rangers. The Mike Forces were also converted to Border Rangers. The CIDG programme was officially terminated on 31

An A Team of 3rd SFGA on a 1966 exercise in Colorado. They are wearing a mix of uniforms including old type tropical fatigues, one-piece coveralls, and OG 107 fatigues. (US Army)

December 1970. The reconnaissance projects were closed down between 1970 and 1972. The 5th SFGA itself was folded down as troops were rotated home. The colours of the 5th SFGA were returned to Ft Bragg on 3 March 1971, and the group was reformed using the assets of the 6th SFGA.

Other SF personnel were to remain in Vietnam a little longer, however. MACV-SOG was inactivated in April 1972. The Strategic Technical Directorate Assistance Team 158 was formed to take its place; though much smaller, it continued SOG's mission until disbanded in March 1973. The US Army Vietnam Individual Training Group (UITG) was formed in February 1971 from SFOD B-36 (the former 3rd Mike Force). Its mission was to train Cambodian infantry battalions and return them to Cambodia to combat the Khmer Rouge. In May 1972 UITG was redesignated Forces Armées Nationales Khmer Training Command (FANK) and continued the same mission until disbanded in

November 1972. SF personnel were to return to Vietnam in 1973–75 as members of the Joint Casualty Resolution Center.

In addition to Vietnam, SF conducted other operations in South-East Asia. The White Star Mobile Training Teams in Laos were just one: a major operation was also conducted in Thailand. Company D (Augmented), 1st SFGA was activated on 15 April 1966 at Ft Bragg and was relocated to Thailand in October. The 46th SF Company was activated on 15 April 1967 in Lopburi, Thailand using the assets of Company D, 1st SFGA. It was responsible for training and advising the Royal Thai Army SF, Rangers, and Border Police. It also conducted various special operations into Laos and Cambodia; and acted as advisers to the Thai 'Queen's Cobras' Regiment and 'Black Panther' Division, which were sent to Vietnam. On 3 March 1972 the assets of the 46th Company were used to form 3rd Battalion, 1st SFGA, at the time a classified designation; it actually had the cover designation of US Army SF, Thailand. After leaving Thailand the unit was inactivated at Ft Bragg on 27 March 1974. It was never physically part of the 1st SFGA.

A member of the 7th SFGA checks out a diver wearing the old type wet suit and a two-tank SCUBA system at Ft Bragg, 1968. (US Army)

Since Vietnam

The post-Vietnam era saw many cutbacks in the strength of the Army, and SF did not escape intact. The 3rd SFGA was inactivated on 1 December 1969, followed by the 6th in 1971. The 5th and 7th SFGAs were to assume their African and Middle Eastern responsibilities. The 10th SFGA was moved from Germany to Ft Devens, Massachusetts in September 1969, but its Company A (redesignated 1st Battalion in 1972) remained at Bad Tölz, and the group as a whole still retained the European mission. Other SF units were also to remain in Germany. SF Detachment Europe had been activated on 11 July 1968 to provide command and control of SF elements there. Another was the 39th SF Detachment (redesignated a company in 1972) which had been activated on 1 September 1965. The 8th SFGA was inactivated on 30 June 1972 and its assets used to form the 3rd Battalion, 7th SFGA which continued with the former's Latin American mission. The 1st SFGA was inactivated at Ft Bragg on 28 June 1974 leaving only SF Detachment Korea in that part of the world.

Besides the reduction of units, there were substantial manning cuts in the remaining ones. The SF Training Group was reorganised into the Institute for Military Assistance Student Battalion in 1972. (The Special Warfare Center had been redesignated the Institute for Military Assistance on 25 July 1969, and this title was to set the tone for SF operations for several years to come.) SF began to assume a low profile, which it would maintain until the early 1980s. Missions continued however, with the major emphasis on Latin America, although Europe and Africa were also to see SF teams. SF also began to undertake civic action missions in the States, among them 'SPARTAN' (Special Proficiency at Rugged Training and Nation Building) directed towards American Indians.

The threat of the terrorist emerged in the 1970s. The US responded to this by forming 1st SFOD D on 20 July 1978 at Ft Bragg. 'Delta Force's' mission is counter-terrorism, and is under the Joint Special Operations Command. Another counter-terrorist unit was 'Blue Light', formed in 1977 by 5th SFGA and disbanded the following year: it was an interim

Ranger, psychological operations, and civil affairs units. The Institute for Military Assistance was redesignated the Special Warfare Center once more on 1 April 1983. On 15 March 1984 the first elements of the 1st SFGA were reactivated at Ft Bragg and deployed to Okinawa. The remainder of the group was activated on 2 September 1984, with the 1st Bn. on Okinawa and the remainder at Ft Lewis, Washington. It assumed its old area of responsibility.

A series of exercises designed to test the deployment of the Rapid Deployment Force were conducted in Egypt from 1982 to 1984. These were known as Exercise 'Bright Star' and elements of the 5th SFGA have taken part in all of them. Elements of 1st Bn., 7th SFGA have been in Honduras since June 1983, training Salvadorian and Honduran troops in counterinsurgency methods. Other SF units are currently concentrating on strategic reconnaissance and direct action missions.

Organisation

Since the beginning, the group has been the principal organisation upon which SF units have been based. Though there have been major reorganisations, the detachment or team concept of internal organisation has remained basically the same. The group has always been commanded by a colonel.

The 10th Special Forces Group (Airborne) was organised under Table of Organization and Equipment (TOE) 33-510, which was approved on 14 May 1952. It consisted of a Headquarters and Headquarters Company (HHC) which controlled a large number of different functionally organised Special Forces Operational Detachments (SFOD). The group at this time had no organic aviation support and required additional service support elements to be fully functional. There was also no Communications Company at this time. The key to group organisation and the concept behind the SFODs was flexibility in organisation, so that tailoring for specific mission requirements could be accomplished with ease. The actual number of SFODs assigned to a given group at any given time will vary.

The HHC consisted of the staff sections and

Two methods of rappelling are demonstrated by 6th SFGA NCOs in Georgia. The lower man, with an AN/PRC-74B radio, is executing the standard rappel while the other conducts an 'Australian' rappel. (US Army)

unit organised for possible deployment until Delta Force was fully operational. Delta Force attempted to rescue the American hostages held in the US Embassy in Iran in April 1980. Delta elements also took part in the Grenada invasion in October 1983.

The early 1980s began to see a re-emergence of interest in special operations in the US military. SF began a relatively fast recovery with this new rediscovery of its capabilities. Unit manning authorisations were increased, new equipment was developed, and levels of training raised. The 1st Special Operations Command was activated at Ft Bragg on 1 October 1982. Its mission is to standardise training, and it is responsible for the preparation, employment, and sustaining of all US Army special operations forces, which includes SF,

A mixed assortment of uniforms are worn by personnel of the 8th SFGA while returning from a counter-guerrilla exercise in the Panama Canal Zone, early 1970s. (US Army)

support elements required for the command and control and service support of the SFODs. All radio contact with deployed teams was maintained by a Communications Section only, which could be augmented by additional personnel and equipment in wartime.

SFODs FD, FC, and FB were deployable to the area of operations for the command and control of SFODs FA. These were, and are, commonly referred to as D, C, B, and A Teams. D, C, and B Teams each had six officers and 18 NCOs. Each team had its own complete staff of officers and NCOs, plus NCOs who gave it the same basic capabilities as an A Team.

Directly under the group was a single SFOD FD (Area). It could be deployed to the area of operations if necessary, and was commanded by the Group Commander.

Also directly under the group were three SFODs FC (District A) each commanded by a lieutenant colonel. Guerrilla units were to be organised on a

district basis. This C Team could control from two to five B Teams and their subordinate A Teams. The C Team was normally responsible for the control of operations in a given country. In garrison the C Team was augmented by an Administrative Detachment AB (Battalion), together forming a provisional battalion headquarters for four or five B Teams and their subordinate A Teams. The detachment, consisting of two officers (one a warrant) and six enlisted men, provided administrative and supply functions as well as the operation of a motor pool.

Two to five SFODs FB (District B) could be attached to each C Team, depending upon the mission requirements. Anywhere from four to ten or more A Teams could be attached to each of these B Teams, which were each commanded by a major. While a C Team was responsible for the operations within a designated country, the B Team was responsible for a given region within that country. An Administrative Detachment AA (Company) would be attached to the B Team in garrison to enable it to act as a provisional company headquarters. This consisted of one warrant officer and 12 enlisted men, and provided administrative, supply, and mess support. In event of deployment of the SFODs, both the Admin. Detachments AA and AB would revert to group control and augment the logistical support functions of the HHC.

The SFOD FA (Regiment), or A Team, was and is the heart of all SF missions and operations. It was originally intended to be capable of organising, equipping, training, and advising an indigenous guerrilla force of company, battalion, or regimental size, up to 1,500 guerrillas. The original A Team consisted of two officers and 13 NCOs. Due to strength reductions at different times they could be found with an authorised strength as low as one officer and five NCOs. Regardless of its authorised strength, the A Team could be split, enabling it to function on two separate missions if necessary. The concept of the A Team was based on the OSS Operational Groups, which consisted of four officers and 30 NCOs trained in speciality skills. They too were able to split and operate separately.

A full-strength A Team in **1958** consisted of:

Team Leader	. . .	Captain
Executive Officer	. . .	1st Lieutenant
Team Sergeant	. . .	Master Sergeant
Weapons Specialists (four)	. . .	Sergeant 1st Class
Demolitions Specialists (four)	. . .	Specialist 2nd Class
Medic	. . .	Master Sergeant
Radio Operators (two)	. . .	Sergeant and Specialist 3rd Class
Radio Repairman	. . .	Sergeant

National Guard and Reserve SF units were first formed in 1959. They were not organised in a group structure at that time, but the same organisational principles were present. The SF units in the West Virginia Army National Guard will serve as an example. Though they were under the control of a D Team, they were not collectively assigned to any given unit: they were merely a grouping of SFODs organised under TOE 33-510R. Located in three West Virginia communities, they comprised the 170th SFOD FD; 101st SFOD FC; 166th Admin. Det. AA; 165th SFOD FA; 167th–169th SFOD FA; 171st–176th SFOD FA. In 1961 the D Team was expanded to form the basis for HHC, 16th SFGA.

The C Team became the group's Company A, to which the expansion of some existing A Teams also contributed. Additional detachments were formed and other A Teams expanded to form Company B; and the group's Company C was formed from existing SFODs in North Carolina.

In 1960 the SFGA underwent its first major reorganisation under TOE 31-105D. A number of internal changes increased the group's capabilities, reducing reliance on outside support, though certain types of support attachments were still required. The group HHC was expanded by increasing the number of organic service support elements. This made it more self-sufficient, but it still required some augmentation. An SF Signal Company was added, greatly improving the group's ability to maintain communications with its deployed SFODs, higher headquarters, and supporting units. It also provided communications equipment maintenance and photographic processing support.

An SF Aviation Company was added in 1963. For the first time—and all too briefly—the group had its own organic aviation support to provide limited air infiltration and exfiltration, resupply, reconnaissance, fire support, command and control, and communications relay. Authorised aircraft were four U-10 *Heliocourier* light single-engine short-take-off-and-landing aircraft; two CV-2B *Caribou* light twin-engine transports; four CH-34C *Choctaw* cargo helicopters, and two UH-1 *Huey* utility helicopters. The Aviation Companies were inactivated in 1965, to furnish aircraft to either the 1st Cavalry Division when it was converted to the airmobile rôle or to aviation units in Vietnam. The company was still part of the TOE, but none were ever again formed, forcing SF to rely on attached aviation units. National Guard and Reserve groups never received an Aviation Company.

Normally a group consisted of four lettered SF Companies, but anywhere from two to five could be assigned. The 'F' and parenthetical titles were also dropped from the designation of the SFODs in the 1960s. A company contained the following:

SFOD C (Company Headquarters)
Administrative Detachment (attached to the C Team)
SFODs B (three)
SFODs A (12, with four attached to each B Team)

The B and C Teams still acted as command and control elements for deployed SFODs. Both were deployable into the area of operations, but the C Team had less ability to conduct some of the same operational functions as an A Team. The C Team consisted of six officers and 12 NCOs. In conjunction with the two officers and 13 enlisted men of the Admin. Detachment, it doubled as the Company Headquarters in garrison. The B Team had six officers and 17 NCOs. It additionally had the full capabilities of an A Team. In garrison it functioned in much the same manner as a platoon headquarters for its subordinate A Teams.

The A Team was reduced to two officers and 12 NCOs. The reason for the change was to take full advantage of having two specialists in each skill, and to enhance its ability to split into two elements for the conduct of separate missions. Minor changes in duty position titles were made during this period, but the **1965** titles listed below provide a common example. As within any military organisation, the use of official terms is not always the case, and SF is no exception. The commonly used titles for duty positions are given in parenthesis following the official titles:

Detachment Commander (Team Leader)	. . . Captain
Executive Officer (XO or, jokingly, 'Excess Officer')	. . . 1st Lieutenant
Operations Sergeant (Team Sergeant)	. . . Master Sergeant
Heavy Weapons Leader (Heavy Weapons Man)	. . . Sergeant 1st Class
Intelligence Sergeant (Intel Sergeant)	. . . Sergeant 1st Class
Light Weapons Leader (Light Weapons Man)	. . . Sergeant 1st Class
Medical Specialist (Senior or Team Medic)	. . . Sergeant 1st Class
Radio Operator Supervisor (Senior Radio Operator)	. . . Sergeant 1st Class
Assistant Medical Specialist (Junior Medic)	. . . Staff Sergeant
Demolitions Sergeant (Engineer Sergeant)	. . . Staff Sergeant
Chief Radio Operator (Junior Radio Operator)	. . . Sergeant
Combat Demolitions Specialist (Demo Man)	. . . Specialist 5

From late **1968** a somewhat different A Team organisation, with 14 men, was employed by the 5th SFGA in Vietnam, the better to answer the needs of its counterinsurgency rôle:

Vietnam veterans assigned to the 6th SFGA crossing a three-rope bridge at Camp Mackall, North Carolina. The two in the rear wear tiger-stripes while the one in the centre wears a Mike Force beret of the same pattern. (US Army)

The old type tree penetration suit is worn by an A Team waiting to board their infiltration aircraft for insertion into Uwharrie National Forest, North Carolina, early 1970s. (US Army)

Detachment Commander	. . .	Captain
Executive Officer	. . .	1st Lieutenant
Civic Action/Psychological Operations Officer	. . .	1st Lieutenant
Operations Sergeant	. . .	Master Sergeant
Heavy Weapons Leader	. . .	Sergeant 1st Class
Intelligence Sergeant	. . .	Sergeant 1st Class
Light Weapons Leader	. . .	Sergeant 1st Class
Medical Specialist	. . .	Sergeant 1st Class
Radio Operator Supervisor	. . .	Sergeant 1st Class
Assistant Medical Specialist	. . .	Staff Sergeant
Demolitions Sergeant	. . .	Sergeant 1st Class
Chief Radio Operator	. . .	Sergeant
Assistant Intelligence Sergeant	. . .	Sergeant
Civic Action/Psychological Operations Specialist	. . .	Specialist 5

National Guard and Reserve SF units were formed into groups in 1961, and were organised under the same basic structure with some exceptions. Initially they had anywhere from one to four SF companies (two or three was the norm). They had no Aviation Company, and did not receive a Signal Company until 1966. The reorganisation of that year reduced total strength to two National Guard and two Reserve SF groups, with elements scattered throughout different states. These groups were not usually authorised a full complement of A and B Teams.

Due to the detachment designation of the SFGAs' organic sub-units, a problem was often encountered by SF officers when credit for command time was given. The C Team was commanded by a lieutenant-colonel and the B Team by a major (a lieutenant-colonel in Vietnam from the late 1960s); but the unit they commanded was still designated a detachment, which in the US Army is defined as a unit organised as a company, but with a strength of under 80. As far as many in the Department of the Army were concerned, an A

Team commander was nothing more than a glorified squad leader, even though he could command a battalion of indigenous troops with all of its responsibilities. In effect, some SF NCOs and junior officers often served on the level of captains, majors, and lieutenant-colonels with indigenous troops in the field. Not only were the careers of serving SF officers being damaged: this handicap dissuaded many other officers from seeking duty in SF. For these reasons and others, a major internal reorganisation was made in the SFGA's TOE in 1970, although it was not put into practice until **1972** as TOE 31-105H:

The HHC was reduced in size, with many of its elements reassigned to the new Service Company. The HHC now had only the staff and planning elements it required to provide effective command and control of the group.

The SF Signal Company was changed only slightly. This was due primarily to improved equipment being introduced.

A new unit, the SF Service Company, was formed. This greatly expanded the group's capability for logistical and service support. It also reintroduced much-needed organic aviation support with U-10 *Heliocourier* fixed-wing and UH-1 *Huey* rotary-wing utility aircraft. The U-10s have since been withdrawn due to age and have not been replaced.

An SF Combat Intelligence Company was added in the late 1970s. The SFGA had previously had to rely on attached Military Intelligence Detachments for their extensive intelligence requirements; in Vietnam the 5th SFGA had ten such detachments assigned to it. The addition of this unit greatly increased the group's operational capabilities.

Initially the group was also authorised an SF Support Battalion Headquarters to control the Service and Signal Companies; but it was determined that the group HHC could control all support units, and this was phased out in the mid-1970s.

Rather than lettered companies, the group was now organised into three numbered battalions. An overall decrease of B and C Teams was realised, as well as a slight increase in A Teams. In addition, the C Teams are now capable of being deployed (when augmented from the Signal, Service, and Intelligence Companies) with less dependence upon group, and can operate a separate forward operations base. The SF Battalion is composed of:

SFOD C (Battalion Headquarters and Headquarters Detachment)
SF Companies (three, designated A, B, C) with each containing:
SFOD B (Company Headquarters)
SFODs A (six)

An NCO accompanies a Montagnard Village Defense Corps patrol in the Vietnamese highlands, January 1963. He wears the OG 107 fatigues with M1945 jungle boots, and is armed with the M1A1 carbine. The Montagnards wear a mixture of ARVN olive green and black uniforms, the latter being standard issue to the Village Defense Corps. They are armed with M1 carbines, and the radio operator carries an AN/PRC-10. (US Army)

The C Team is basically the same as the pre-1972 version, having eight officers and 14 NCOs, and functions in the same manner. The B Team now consists of only two officers and three NCOs. It acts solely as a command and control element. When deployed to the area of operations it will co-locate with one of its A Teams for security and support. In garrison it acts as a company headquarters for its subordinate A Teams. During the period of post-Vietnam manning cuts, there were often only four A Teams. This was done to prevent reducing the strength of all A Teams.

The A Team remains basically the same, with only slight changes in duty position titles. Due to lessons learned in Vietnam and elsewhere, the number of indigenous troops that an A Team can train has been reduced to a more realistic 500: a battalion. Rank structure is the same as the 1965 A Team.

Montagnard Mountain Commandos prepare for a reconnaissance mission disguised as local civilians, Plei Yt Commando Training Center, March 1963. The M3A1 submachine guns and grenades were concealed in the rice baskets. The blankets and loin cloths are deep blue with yellow, red and blue braiding and fringing. (US army)

Detachment Commander	Medical NCO
Executive Officer	Radio Op. S'rvisor
Operations Sergeant	SF Engineer Sgt.
Heavy Weapons Leader	Asst. Medic NCO
Asst. Ops. Sgt.	Chief Radio Op.
Light Weapons Leader	SF Engineer

National Guard and Reserve SFGAs were reorganised shortly after the regular groups. Some groups initially had up to six battalions, although some of these had only a headquarters. They now have three battalions each and their B Teams contain five A Teams. National Guard and Reserve groups do not have a Combat Intelligence Company, but rather a Military Intelligence Detachment. These are all Army Reserve units. The plan is to reorganise them as Combat Intelligence Companies in the near future.

In the early 1960s a new organisation, the Special Action Force (SAF), began to be formed. Its function was to provide assistance to developing countries in the form of counterinsurgency training for its armed forces and assistance in improving the quality of life for rural inhabitants.

The SFGA was the principal unit around which the area-oriented SAFs were built. Additional units capable of providing military training and civil assistance were added as required. SAFs are now referred to as Security Assistance Forces, and are not currently formed as such, but can be when required. Organised SAFs in the late 1960s and early 1970s were: SAF Asia (1st SFGA); SAF Africa (3rd SFGA); SAF Middle East (6th SFGA); SAF Latin America (8th SFGA); SAF Europe (10th SFGA).

The organisation of SAFs varied due to the requirements of their assigned area of responsibility. The 10th SFGA had almost no attached units, while the others had a varied mix which might include: Psychological Operations Battalion or Company; Civil Affairs Battalion or Company; and Military Intelligence, Army Security Agency, Military Police, Engineer, and Medical Detachments.

There are a number of future changes in store for the SFGA. Most of these involve improving support capabilities and easing manpower constraints. It is planned that the Combat Intelligence Company be reorganised into a Combat Electronic Warfare Intelligence (CEWI) Company combining the standard military intelligence disciplines with the electronic warfare and communications intelligence capabilities of the now dissolved Army Security Agency. The Reserve companies (now detachments) will likewise be reorganised.

It is also planned for a Special Operations Aviation Group to be activated in the future. The groups may again lose their organic aviation, but detachments from the Aviation Group will be co-located with SF and other special operations units. Procurement of additional aircraft, such as the UV-18 *Twin Otter* medium utility short-take-off-and-landing transport, is also planned.

The A Team, too, will go through a number of changes. Lieutenants as Executive Officers are being phased out, to be replaced by warrant officers promoted from senior SF NCOs. This has the advantage of conserving commissioned officers of whom there has often been a shortage in SF. It also provides an opportunity to retain experienced NCOs who might otherwise leave the service. It is currently planned that the A Team will be reduced to two officers and eight NCOs in 1988.

Selection and Training

The standards for SF selection have always been high; although they have been raised and lowered as demanded by strength requirements over the years, the overall prerequisites have changed little. These take into account an individual's background (both civilian and military), mental aptitude, physical ability, and certain military administrative requirements. SF troops are triple

volunteers—for the Army, for airborne, and for SF. An individual must complete Basic Training, Advanced Individual Training (where he is trained in his Military Occupation Speciality or MOS), and the three week Airborne Course (where he becomes a qualified parachutist). An individual slated for SF training will usually be trained as an infantryman. Individuals who have been in the service must complete the Airborne Course before attending SF training. Officers must meet the same basic requirements as enlisted men, and must have completed their basic branch training.

SF training begins at Ft Bragg, where the students are assigned to the Special Forces School to attend the SF Qualification Course, or 'Q' Course. The 'Q' Course (formerly SF Tactics and Techniques) is divided into three phases. Details, training emphasis, locations, etc. have changed, but the overall content of today's 'Q' Course is much the same as it was 20 years ago. Attrition is high, although not as high as it was in the early days.

The goal of Phase I is to teach the common skills required by all SF troops, to test them physically and mentally, and to eliminate those lacking the required motivation and initiative. The skills concentrated upon are land navigation, patrolling, and survival (methods of instruction were taught in Phase I, but are now covered in Phase II). Physical testing is accomplished by distance runs, rucksack marches, and confidence and obstacle courses. This four week phase also includes a couple of parachute

Members of Detachment A-222, Dong Tre Strike Force, relax after the discovery of a large arms cache in Phu Yen Province, February 1965. They wear the spotted camouflage uniform. (US Army)

Chinese Nungs of the 3rd Mike Force returning from Operation 'Golden Gate', November 1966. They are armed with M2 carbines and M1918A2 BARs. (US Army)

jumps, a period of five days without food (while all training continues), tactical patrolling exercises and land navigation courses. The green beret is awarded upon completion of Phase I.

Phase II is where the students learn their SF speciality training committees. Physical training continues at a fast pace. This phase is primarily academic, although 'hands-on', performance-oriented training is conducted to the extent possible. Emphasis is also placed on being able to teach these skills to others. Except for the medical course, Phase II is eight weeks long.

The engineer course covers conventional and unconventional (home made) explosives; demolitions techniques; obstacle, light building and bridge construction; and engineer reconnaissance. Some SF engineers are sent to the Army's Engineer School for additional training such as heavy construction equipment operation.

The weapons course is divided into light and heavy weapons. The light weapons portion trains the student to operate and disassemble dozens of small arms: handguns, rifles, sub-machine guns, machine guns, grenade launchers, etc. Current and obsolete US, Allied, and Communist weapons are studied—the older weapons especially, as guerrillas will usually be armed with these. The heavy weapons portion deals with mortars, recoilless rifles, and infantry rocket launchers. The mortar training predominates.

The communications course was at one time 16 weeks long. It is shorter now due to the simplicity of the newer radios, their ease of repair, and less time being spent on radio theory. Operation of SF radios and burst message devices, cryptographic systems, manual Morse Code, and the many clandestine SF communications techniques are covered.

The 25 week medical course is the most difficult one, although at one time it lasted 39 weeks. It is divided into 13 weeks at the Army's Academy of Health Sciences at Ft Sam Houston, Texas followed by six weeks of on-the-job training at an Army hospital, and then six weeks of patient care and lab techniques. Regardless of the course's length the SF medic is extensively trained in advanced field

The commander (right) and some NCOs of Detachment A-302 of the 3rd Mike Force, after receiving Silver Stars for their part in Operation 'Attleboro', December 1966. (P. Lopez)

medical procedures, and is highly respected by his fellow team members.

The operations and intelligence course is for senior NCOs and covers the many aspects of mission planning, and UW and special operations intelligence techniques. It is not conducted during Phase II, but taken by team operations sergeants.

Phase III is where the students can put into practice all that they have learned at the team level. During this phase's four weeks they learn the basics of UW operations and mission planning. It is completed by a two week UW exercise. Students plan and otherwise prepare for the mission, and then parachute into Uwharrie National Forest north of Ft Bragg. Each team links up with its guerrilla group (made up of instructor-led SF students). The student team will organise and train the guerrillas and then assist them in the execution of a raid plus other UW tasks. The students graduate upon accomplishing Phase III, and are now 'flash qualified'.

Officers were initially trained in a manner similar to enlisted men with much of the training being accomplished within the units. In 1956 the SF Officer Course was established; this was always a 12 week course. It covered many of the same areas as the enlisted Phases I and III with the addition of the many planning, operational, and intelligence aspects of UW and special operations. Since 1981, however, the officers have been integrated with the enlisted men, conducting Phases I and III with them and undertaking their own Phase II training.

Once assigned to an SF unit the trooper has ample opportunities for additional training—in fact his training never really ends. Even in Vietnam, from the late 1960s, SF troops went through a two week Combat Orientation Course conducted by the Recondo School. Additional individual and team training are conducted continuously. This includes MOS cross-training and language qualification (not every man is trained in a second language, contrary to popular opinion). Advanced training in SCUBA and free-fall parachuting are also conducted by selected individuals. Other Army courses are also available such as the Ranger; Pathfinder; Jumpmaster; and Survival, Evasion, Resistance and Escape Courses. Unit training encompasses exercises in different terrain and weather environments.

Insignia

The best-known SF insignia is the green beret (officially, 'Beret, Man's, Wool, Rifle Green'). The story of its adoption is long and involved, but may be summarised as follows:

The idea of the beret as SF's official headwear is attributed to Captains Herbert Brucker and Roger Pezzelle of the 10th SFGA. Berets of various colours had been worn as field headwear by a small number of individuals since the group had been formed. In the late summer of 1952 these two captains came up with the idea of a camouflage beret for field and everyday wear along with a camouflage uniform. Capt. Pezzelle ordered some green berets from Canada, as camouflage ones were not manufactured. Before the berets arrived the 10th SFGA deployed to Germany. When the berets arrived at Ft Bragg members of the 77th SFGA began to wear them and more were purchased. The 10th found out about this, and ordered berets from a firm in Munich. They were strictly illegal at this time. Over the next two years the berets began to be worn more and more openly at both Bad Tölz and Ft Bragg. The troops were always prepared to switch to a regulation field cap when high ranking 'outsiders' appeared in their unit area.

In late 1954 an attempt was made to legalise the beret. At Ft Bragg Col. Edson Raff, commander of the Psychological Warfare Center, requested authorisation, but a reply was never received. He took it upon himself to approve the Canadian-made beret for local wear on the last day of 1955, as a test 'to determine its suitability'. The post commander banned it the following year, however. The troops continued to wear it in the field, but it was not worn openly at Ft Bragg again until 1961. Col. William Ekman, new commander of the 10th SFGA, granted approval for local wear, and assigned Capt. Brucker as the procurement officer. French-made berets were purchased in 1955. The 10th was able to continue the wear of the beret through the remainder of the 1950s with few problems. The 1st SFGA also wore the beret on a locally approved basis after its formation in 1957. Several attempts were made to secure official sanction during the late 1950s, but all were disapproved.

Brig.Gen. William Yarborough, commander of the Special Warfare Center in 1960–65, was instrumental in finally securing approval of the beret. The general could see the value of functional uniforms and distinctive insignia for specialised units. During World War II, as the test officer of the Airborne Command, he developed the design of the

An NCO of Detachment A-301 coaches a CIDG trainee in use of the M79 grenade launcher at Camp Trang Sup, the III Corps CIDG Training Center, in March 1967. The unit scarf is medium blue. A CIDG NCO of Mobile Guerrilla Force Co. 957 looks on (right). On his shoulder can be seen the insignia depicted in close-up, which is typical of locally produced CIDG insignia. (CIDG—US Army, patch—C. B. Smyth)

jump boot, parachutist's badge, and paratrooper uniform. The boots (though now black) and the badge are still worn. In 1960 he used the paratrooper uniform as a model for the lightweight jungle fatigues which have been a standard for US Army field uniforms ever since. The general's West Point classmate, Maj.Gen. Chester Clifton, was the military aide to President Kennedy; and it was through him that approval of the beret was granted by the President on 25 September 1961. When the President visited Ft Bragg in October 1961 to review Special Forces the troopers were wearing the beret, and it was officially entered into the uniform regulations on 10 December.

A member of Co. D, 1st SFGA accompanying the Royal Thai Army on an operation, March 1967. This was prior to the redesignation of this unit as 46th SF Company. (US Army)

Beret badges, flashes and bars

During the early 1950s the parachutist badge, or 'jumpwings', was worn on the beret, positioned over the left temple. The 77th SFGA, and later the 1st SFGA, added the SF airborne background trimming. These are more commonly referred to as 'jumpwing backgrounds' or 'ovals'. They are worn as a backing for the parachutist badge as an additional means of unit identification. They are normally worn on service-type uniforms, and sometimes on headwear. Officers in the 77th sometimes wore their rank insignia beneath the wings.

The 10th SFGA initially wore jumpwings without the background. In 1955 they took a different track when Capt. Pezzelle designed the 'Trojan Horse' badge: a large silver-coloured badge depicting a Trojan horse superimposed over a lightning bolt and enclosed within a shield-shaped winged frame. The Trojan horse and lightning bolt were to influence many future SF insignia. The badge was worn over the left temple; officers wore their rank insignia forward of the badge. The group commander approved its wear on 25 September 1955; delivered in January 1956, it was worn until the 'flash' was issued in 1962.

Beret flashes are an important symbol in SF, serving to identify groups and other units and organisations. The flash system was developed by Gen. Yarborough in 1961 in anticipation of approval of the beret. The original flashes were made of felt and measured approximately $1\frac{5}{8}$ ins. wide by 2 ins. high. Felt flashes were used, in some cases, until the mid-1960s, but in the early 1960s the embroidered flash began to appear. These were generally larger, and the standard flash size is $1\frac{7}{8}$ ins. wide and $2\frac{1}{4}$ ins. high. Other materials such as naugahyde (artificial leather) and plastic have been used. The flash is worn above the left eye; enlisted men wear their unit crest on the flash while officers wear their rank insignia. The 'full-flash', as it is called, was formerly worn only by personnel who were fully SF-qualified. This was changed in 1984.

It is a little-known fact that the green beret is worn by all personnel assigned to SF units whether they are SF qualified or not. Men who are not SF-qualified, some of whom may not even be airborne-qualified, can be found in Group Headquarters and Service Companies, and Administrative Detach-

Typical Khmer CIDG Strikers in III Corps Tactical Zone, late 1960s. The unarmed man is probably the company adjutant (first sergeant). (US Army)

ments. They wore, until 1984, what was officially referred to as the 'SF recognition bar', more commonly known as the 'half-flash', 'striker bar', 'candy stripe' or 'candy bar'. These were introduced in the mid-1960s, and measure $1\frac{7}{8}$ ins. long and $\frac{1}{2}$ in. wide. These troops originally wore only their crest or officer rank insignia on the beret. The candy stripe, adopted so that the wearer's group could be identified, was worn beneath the crest or rank insignia. Some units never did have a candy stripe. In 1984, after the authorisation of the SF qualification tab, it was directed that non-SF-qualified personnel would now wear the 'full-flash'. This decision met with much opposition, but the candy stripe was eliminated.

Crests

Distinctive unit insignia, incorrectly but more commonly referred to as crests, are worn by all personnel to identify their parent organisation. Enlisted men wear them on the beret, and they and officers wear them on the shoulder straps of service uniforms. These are enamelled metal badges, usually just over one inch high.

The 10th and 77th SFGAs were authorised crests after they were activated. The 1st SFGA was authorised a crest in the late 1950s, but it was never worn on the uniform.

On 15 April 1960 the 1st Special Forces was activated as the parent organisation for all SF units. A new crest was approved on 24 May 1960. The 1st SF crest consists of a black scroll with the SF motto in silver, DE OPPRESSO LIBER—'Free the Oppressed'. Two crossed silver arrows are superimposed on the scroll, and represent the branch-of-service insignia of the 1st Special Service Force. On the arrows is a point-up silver Fairbairn fighting knife as used by the 1st Special Service Force.

The Psychological Warfare School received a crest on 28 November 1952, approved for wear by the Special Warfare Center on 18 September 1957. The new 1st Special Operations Command was authorised its crest in July 1983.

Shoulder insignia

Initially the 10th and 77th SFGAs wore the shoulder sleeve insignia (commonly called patches) of the World War II Airborne Command. This patch was worn by SF as a cover from 1952–55. It was reinstated as the insignia of the 'Airborne Command for wear by certain classified units', to quote the file, on 10 April 1952.

The Special Forces patch was approved on 22

Members of the 5th Mike Force board a C-123 transport on 2 April 1967 for the first Mike Force airborne assault. Almost 350 CIDG and USSF jumped to secure a site for a Strike Force Camp at Bunard. (US Army)

August 1955, and the same letter rescinded the wear of the Airborne Command patch. It was designed by Capt. John W. Frye of the 77th SFGA. The arrowhead represents the 1st Special Service Force and the gold-yellow short sword signifies unconventional warfare. The three lightning bolts of the same colour represent the three means of infiltration—land, sea, and air. The teal blue colour designates 'branch unassigned', as SF is not assigned to a given branch.

Originally an Airborne tab was not authorised for wear with the patch, but it was worn without exception. The 10th used one of gold-yellow on teal blue, while the 1st and 77th wore a gold-yellow-on-black tab. Both could be found being worn in the different groups due to cross-reassignment of personnel. On 20 November 1958 the gold-yellow-on-black Airborne tab was officially authorised for wear. This patch is *never* worn upside down as is sometimes reported!

The Psychological and Special Warfare Centers wore the Third US Army patch from 1952 until March 1962. From March to October 1962 the

Continental Army Command patch was worn, consisting of (from the bottom) red, white, and blue horizontal stripes. A white-on-blue Airborne tab was worn with both patches. The Special Warfare Center was authorised its own patch on 22 October 1962. It has a black background bordered in gold-yellow, with a white lamp in the centre superimposed over crossed gold-yellow arrows. Issuing from the lamp are red flames edged gold-yellow. A gold-yellow-on-black Airborne tab has been worn at times and not authorised at others. The 1st Special Operations Command received a patch in July 1983.

The SF qualification tab was authorised in July 1983 to identify SF-qualified personnel. It is worn on the left shoulder above the individual's unit patch. If an individual is both SF- and Ranger-qualified he may wear only one tab, but can wear each on different uniforms.

The Plates

A1: Captain, FA Detachment Commander, 10th SFGA; Bad Tölz, West Germany, 1956
This officer wears winter semi-dress uniform, often

1: Captain, 10th SFGA;
   Germany, 1956
2: M/Sergeant, 1st SFGA;
   Okinawa, 1960
3: Brig. Gen. Yarborough;
   Ft. Bragg, 1961

A

1: HALO parachutist, 7th SFGA; Ft. Bragg, 1973
2: HALO parachutist, 5th SFGA; Ft. Bragg, 1978
3: PRTS; Ft. Bragg, 1982

B

1: Pfc, SF Training Group; Ft. Bragg, 1968
2: Pfc, USAIMA Student Bn.; Pope AFB, 1983
3: CTU-2/A High Speed Aerial Delivery Container

C

1: Cpl., 77th SFGA; Uwharrie National Forest, 1955
2: Sgt., 6th SFGA; Ft. Greely, 1970
3: 1st Lt., 11th SFGA; Camp Drum, 1972

D

1: NCO, Camp Strike Force,
5th SFGA; Vietnam, 1969
2: CIDG Striker, Co. 331;
Chi Linh, Vietnam, 1969
3: S/Sgt., Camp Strike Force,
5th SFGA; Vietnam, 1967

E

1: Sgt. 1st Class, 3rd MSF,
   5th SFGA; Vietnam, 1966
2: Spec. 5, 2nd MSFC,
   5th SFGA; Vietnam, 1969
3: CIDG Striker; Plei Mrong, Vietnam, 1964

F

1: NCO, Recce Team Leader,
   MACV-SOG; Vietnam, 1960s
2: NCO, Project Delta,
   5th SFGA; Vietnam, 1964
3: CIDG Mountain Scout;
   Plei Yt, Vietnam, 1963

G

1: S/Sgt., Detachment A-41, 46th SF Co.; Thailand, 1972
2: 1st Lt., Det. A-45, 46th SF Co.; Thailand, 1972
3: Fulton STAR system

H

1: Sgt. 1st Class,
   TF Ivory Coast; Son Tay,
   North Vietnam, 1970
2: NCO, Delta Force; Desert
   Base One, Iran, 1980

KITD/FOHS

3: NCO SCUBA diver,
   8th SFGA; Panama, 1972

I

1: S/Sgt., 10th SFGA;
   Ft. Devens, 1983
2: Major, 5th SFGA;
   Egypt, 1982
3: Sgt. Maj., 1st SOC;
   Ft. Bragg, 1984

J

1

2

3

4

Beret Flashes and Backgrounds – see Plates commentaries:

5

6

7

8

9

10

11

12

13

14

15

16

K

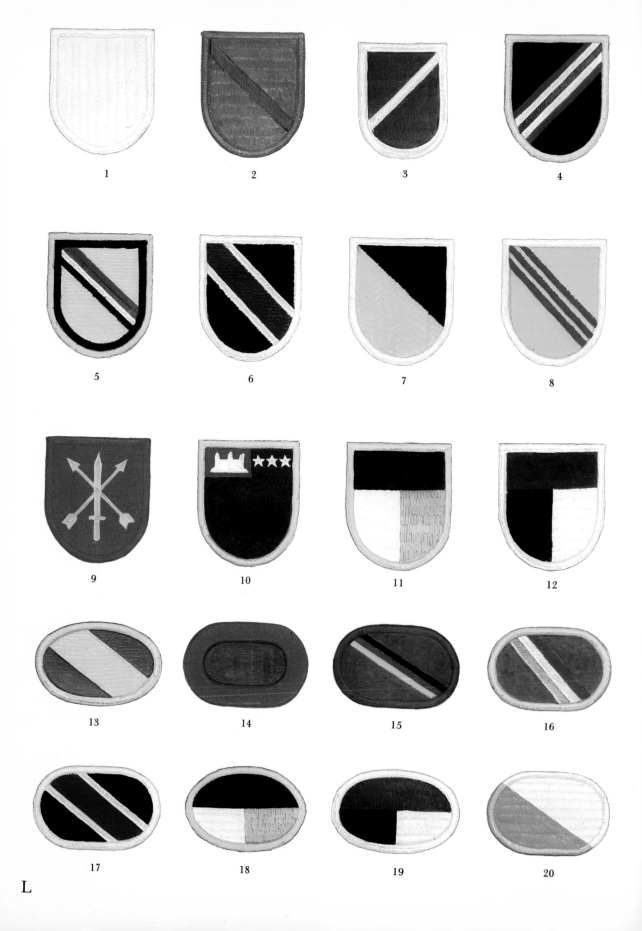

1   2   3   4

5   6   7   8

9   10   11   12

13   14   15   16

17   18   19   20

L

referred to as 'pinks and greens' due to its appearance in bright sunlight. He wears the still-unofficial, German-made 'Munich' beret, which is of a lighter green than the later ones. Over the temple he wears the Group's 'Trojan Horse' badge. The Ranger and unofficial gold-yellow-on-teal-blue Airborne tabs are worn over the newly authorised Special Forces patch.

A2: Master Sergeant, FA Detachment Sergeant, 1st SFGA; Ft Buckner, Okinawa, 1960

The A Team Operations Sergeant, as the senior enlisted man on the team, had the additional duty of 'Team Sergeant'. In a sense he was the first sergeant of the team and was, and is, often referred to as 'Top'. Over his right chest pocket he wears Nationalist Chinese master jumpwings: foreign jumpwings (or other qualification badges) are often worn by US personnel in this position when awarded by Allied units with which they have trained. Members of the 1st SFGA had numerous opportunities to obtain foreign jumpwings, and some individuals had different wings on virtually every uniform. The Army Khaki uniform was available in issue cotton or privately purchased tropical worsted wool; often referred to as 'TWs',

these were much favoured by officers and senior NCOs.

A3: Brigadier General William P. Yarborough, Commandant, US Army Special Warfare Center; Ft Bragg, NC, 1961

President John F. Kennedy, considered by many to be the 'patron saint' of SF, visited Ft Bragg on 12 October 1961 for a demonstration of SF capabilities. It was the first time that SF troopers appeared en masse wearing the green beret with official sanction. When the President stepped from his limousine to be greeted by Gen. Yarborough, he asked, 'Those are very nice. How do you like the green beret?' The general replied, 'They're fine, sir. We've wanted them for a long time.' Later, in a letter to Gen. Yarborough thanking him for SF's efforts, the President wrote, 'I am sure that the Green Beret will be a mark of distinction in the trying times ahead.' Little did he know of the future trials that SF would endure and survive; but one of its longest battles, for the beret, had been won. The camouflage flash was one of a kind and was worn

Camp Binh Than Thon, IV Corps Tactical Zone, Detachment A-413, photographed in 1969. This shows a typical improved Strike Force fighting camp. (US Army)

only by the general. He wears the cotton utility uniform or fatigues. The Third US Army patch with Airborne tab was the authorised insignia for the Special Warfare Center until 1962. The general had been awarded the combat infantryman's badge, but seldom wore it on field uniforms.

B1: NCO, High Altitude–Low Opening Parachutist, 7th SFGA; Ft Bragg, NC, 1973

The High Altitude–Low Opening (HALO) concept was developed by the 77th SFGA in 1957–58, and involves the principles of sport skydiving modified to meet the requirements of military free-fall. Its purpose is to provide a means of parachute insertion into the area of operations, while making it difficult to detect and/or destroy the aircraft due to its extremely high altitude of up to 40,000 feet. The HALO Course is conducted by the Special Warfare Center, as well as by some of the groups in the past. Groups normally maintain some A Teams that are fully HALO-qualified. This jumper is wearing his own jumpsuit and French-made jumpboots—an outfit often worn for training, but not for actual deployment. He wears the MC-3 leather jump helmet with MBU3P oxygen mask: oxygen is required at over 10,000 feet. In the jump aircraft the mask hose is plugged into an on-board oxygen system; just prior to the jump it is connected to the 'bailout' oxygen bottles under the reserve parachute, which provide about 15 minutes of oxygen.

The indigenous members of MACV-SOG's Spike Recon Team California at the Command and Control Central Forward Operations Base, 1969. The teams were designated by states, snakes, and various implements. They wear their team patch on their uniforms. These uniforms were not worn on missions. (Author's collection)

The main parachute assembly is the A/P28-3, which has a 35 ft olive green steerable canopy; this parabolic circular canopy has a large oval steering vent in the back, and steering is accomplished by slip risers. Strapped to his side is an M16A1 rifle with an M203 40 mm grenade launcher. On his shoulder is the patch of the Co. A, 2nd SFGA Sport Parachute Club, his former Army Reserve unit based in Cleveland, Ohio in the early 1960s.

B2: NCO, High Altitude–Low Opening Parachutist, 5th SFGA; Ft Bragg, NC, 1978

This jumper is equipped with the later MC-3 free-fall parachute assembly, which includes the military version of the sport Para-Commander Mark I canopy (pictured in the background). This is a highly manoeuvrable 24 ft canopy, available in olive green or a camouflage pattern. The reserve parachute is an olive green flat circular non-steerable canopy. The rucksack, a large LC-1 ALICE (Advanced Lightweight Individual Carrying Equipment) with an LC-1 frame, is strapped behind the jumper, rather than on the front as in the case of static line jumpers, to allow a more stable free-fall position. Additional team equipment can be dropped in a free-fall bundle with its own parachute and automatic opener. Free-fall jumpers usually manually deploy their parachutes at 2,000 feet; an altimeter is used to determine this altitude. As a back-up the FF-2 automatic ripcord release assembly is used. This soldier carries an M16A1 rifle.

He is wearing a more practical uniform for a mission: camouflage jungle fatigues, probably with long underwear and a field jacket liner underneath to protect him from the cold at high altitudes. Introduced in 1967, this was seldom used by SF in Vietnam, but was extensively worn by 'Stateside' SF units from the early 1970s. He wears the patch of his former Vietnam combat unit on his right shoulder: the 173rd Airborne Brigade.

A further refinement of HALO is the High Altitude–High Opening (HAHO) concept. This involves leaving the aircraft at a very high altitude and opening shortly thereafter. The jumper will then 'fly' his high-performance, ram-air canopy over a considerable distance before selecting his landing site. This allows the aircraft to 'stand off' a safe distance from the area of operations. This technique began to be developed in 1977 during the Off-Set Parachuting Techniques Concept Evaluation Program. A new system known as the Special Operations Advanced Parachute System (SOAPS) is currently under development.

B3: NCO, Parachutist Rough Terrain System, US Army Institute for Military Assistance; Ft Bragg, NC, 1982
The ability of an A Team to parachute into an area considered to be unfavourable for parachute insertion is highly desirable, but somewhat risky. For years SF has used techniques and equipment developed by US Forest Service 'smoke jumpers' for this purpose. This includes the use of penetration suits, and the conduct of rough terrain parachuting courses for landing in heavily wooded, rocky or mountainous areas. The old two-piece penetration suits were of heavy olive green cotton canvas (although white and orange ones have been used in training) with padding at the knees and elbows. There was a leg-bag on the right leg containing a 50 ft lowering rope. A football helmet with a wire mesh faceguard was used. In 1981 the requirement for a new suit was established. This was designated the Parachutist Rough Terrain System (PRTS), and is a one-piece suit made of heavy olive green nylon with pads protecting the neck, armpits, kidneys, elbows, crotch, and knees. A motorcycle-type helmet with a clear plastic face shield is included. Test helmets are white, but once adopted, olive green ones will be issued. The issue of suits in camouflage fabric is also being considered. The suit contains an internal harness to which a leg-bag stowed lowering line system is attached. It is expected to be issued in 1986. An M1950 weapons container is attached to the jumper's parachute harness.

C1: PFC, Student, SF Training Group; Simmons Army Air Field, Ft Bragg, NC, 1968
This SF Student is prepared to jump from a C-119 transport into Camp Mackall for his Phase I Field Training Exercise. He wears cotton fatigues with full-colour insignia: subdued insignia were not introduced until late that year. This was also before the rocker was added to PFC stripes. The trousers are a popular commercial version available in Post Exchanges and referred to as 'ranger' trousers due to the addition of the leg cargo pockets. On his M1

helmet is the old leaf pattern camouflage cover. On the reverse side of the cover is a spotted camouflage pattern of four shades of brown. The rucksack is the nylon, aluminium frame jungle model, which is attached to the jumper upside down. It was extensively used by SF units in the USA, but seldom in Vietnam, as its design limited the number of items that could be attached to the utility belt. About 200 ft above ground the jumper will release the rucksack which will drop below him secured by a 15 ft lowering line; this prevents injury from the heavy rucksack on landing. His weapon is an M14, 7.62 mm NATO rifle. M16A1s were available, but M14s were heavier, so they were issued to students. The main parachute is a static-line-deployed T-10 consisting of an olive green 35 ft parabolic circular non-steerable canopy. The reserve is a white 24 ft flat circular non-steerable canopy.

C2: PFC, Student, US Army Institute for Military Assistance Student Battalion; Pope Air Force Base, NC, 1983
Today's SF Student, prepared for his Phase I ordeal at Camp Mackall; his jump aircraft will be a C-130. He is clothed in the new woodland pattern Battle Dress Uniform (BDU)—see Plate J1. A matching, non-reversible camouflage helmet cover is now issued. The rucksack is the large LC-1 ALICE pack with the later LC-2 frame. Load bearing equipment (LBE) is a mixture of the new nylon ALICE and

Part of Detachment A-502, Co. E, 5th SFGA, an augmented A Team under the Nha Trang Installation Defense Command, late 1969. It operated a half-dozen defensive camps located in a belt around Nha Trang, the 5th SFGA's operations base. (US Army)

cotton canvas M1956 gear. His weapon is an M16A1 rifle in an M1950 weapons container. The main parachute is an MC1-1/B, an olive green 35 ft parabolic circular steerable canopy (pictured in the background). The reserve is now olive green. Both the main and reserve parachute containers are now of nylon rather than the cotton canvas used for the T-10. This system also features a greatly improved harness.

C3: CTU-2/A High Speed Aerial Delivery Container
The CTU-2/A was developed in the late 1970s to provide a means of resupplying A Teams from high speed aircraft. It was an outgrowth of a technique developed in Vietnam, where napalm bomb containers filled with supplies were dropped from fighter aircraft to resupply Mobile Guerrilla Forces and other special operations elements. It can be dropped from jet fighters flying at up to 425 knots from as low as 300 feet. It weighs only 213 lbs and can be loaded with up to 500 lbs of supplies and equipment. Measuring 21 ins. in diameter and 106

ins. long, it is parachute-retarded and re-usable— although, being made of fibreglass and acrylic resin, it can be burned after delivery. The parachute is a white 34 ft ringslot drag canopy. It is shown exposed here, but is normally covered by a tailcone.

D1: Corporal, Weapons Specialist, 77th SFGA; Uwharrie National Forest, NC, 1955
This weapons specialist is presenting a class to 'guerrillas' on the Soviet PPSh-41 sub-machine gun. During this period the 77th was wearing a Canadian-made beret. He wears the herringbone fatigue uniform with an M1953 field jacket. In 1955 the World War II rank chevrons (previously worn until 1948) replaced the small and unpopular gold-yellow and dark blue chevrons.

D2: Sergeant, Demolitions Specialist, 6th SFGA; Ft Greely, AK, 1970
Rappelling is a basic skill for SF troopers. This man wears a wool shirt with field trousers, the trouser counterpart of the field jacket. Climbing boots (usually referred to as 'Chippewas' after the manufacturer), the M1951 field cap (commonly referred to as the patrol cap), and work gloves complete the outfit. Slung over his shoulders are an

SF NCOs and Montagnard Strikers of the 5th Mobile Strike Force, late 1960s. The Americans tended to 'go native' rather quickly once in the field. Captured weapons are being presented to the Americans. (US Army)

Task Force Ivory Coast's Assault Group on a C-130 transport en route between Takhli and Udorn Royal Thai Air Force Bases, 21 November 1970. At Udorn they transloaded to HH-53 helicopters and departed for Son Tay, North Vietnam. The 'criss-crossed' box in the centre is the demolition charge used to breach the prison's wall.

M14 rifle (not standard issue, but sometimes used in exercises) and a non-electric demolitions kit.

D3: 1st Lieutenant, A Detachment Executive Officer, 11th SFGA; Camp Drum, NY, 1972

Operating the team's G-13 hand-cranked generator is one of the less popular chores that members are called upon to perform; it is a standing joke within SF that this is one of the principal duties of the A Team XO. He wears an olive green cold weather parka and field trousers under a two-piece overwhite camouflage suit. The parka has a detachable fur-ruffed hood. The cold weather insulated cap is designed to be worn under the helmet; a woodland camouflage version was introduced in 1983. Three-finger mittens, often referred to as 'triggerfinger' mittens, and rubber insulated boots complete the outfit. The boots are also made in black; known as 'Mickey Mouse' or 'VB' (vapor barrier) boots, they are extremely warm—sometimes too warm, as they are completely airtight. For this reason there is an air release valve on the side to allow for equalisation of pressure when in an aircraft.

E1: NCO, Weapons Specialist, Camp Strike Force, 5th SFGA; Vietnam, 1969

This member of an A Detachment is wearing the later pattern tiger-stripe uniform with a locally purchased jungle hat. The not-too-popular blue and green striped scarf was worn by some members of Co. A, 5th SFGA. It was extremely rare for any insignia to be worn on these uniforms—primarily for security reasons, but also because they only lasted for a few operations. His M16A1 rifle has camouflage tape applied. The LBE is all M1956 cotton canvas equipment. The ammo pouches were designed to hold two M14 magazines, but they could hold four 20-round M16A1 magazines also. Since these magazines were shorter, additional field dressings were often placed in the bottoms to raise the magazines up. One of his four ammo pouches contains such items as a penflare projector, signal mirror, and small marker panel, all used to mark his unit's position for aircraft. The first aid pouch on his suspenders contains a lensatic compass. The indigenous rucksack is being carried (see also under Plate F2). Jungle boots were first issued in 1965.

E2: CIDG Striker, Company 331; Chi Linh Camp Strike Force, III Corps Tactical Zone, Vietnam, 1969

This Striker wears an older version of the tiger-stripes than E1. These are faded, but were originally a lighter shade to begin with. His jungle hat is standard indigenous issue, but has the brim cut down by the camp tailor, a common practice. His boots are the later black canvas, rubber soled 'Bata' boots manufactured by Bata Footwear of Canada. Some CIDG managed to acquire US-made, Asian size jungle and all-leather combat boots. The company scarf, originally red, white and blue, has faded with washing. The CIDG Camp Strike Force patch, authorised in 1968, was normally worn on the left shoulder, but Co. 331 wore it on a red patch

A helicopter extraction using the McGuire rig, predecessor of the STABO system, here employed by members of the 46th SF Company, Thailand, 1971. Lift-off had to be slow to prevent the troops from being slammed into each other as they came off the ground. (S. L. Stanton)

on the chest pocket. He wears M1956 LBE and carries an ARVN rucksack. This latter item was not too popular as it soaked up water, becoming heavier, and its top flap securing straps ran over the top where they often snagged on branches. It was tolerated, though, because of its larger load capacity than the indigenous rucksack. The M2 carbine, .30cal., capable of both semi- and fully-automatic fire, was the principal weapon of the Camp Strike Forces (along with a few M1 rifles, M1918A2 Browning Automatic Rifles, and M79 40mm grenade launchers) until they were replaced en masse by the M16A1 rifle in the spring of 1969.

E3: Staff Sergeant, Medical Specialist, Camp Strike Force, 5th SFGA; Vietnam, 1967

Except when actually conducting operations, when tiger-stripes were worn, SF troopers normally wore the standard jungle fatigues. All authorised insignia were worn on these uniforms. Even after 1968, when subdued insignia were introduced, full-colour embroidered insignia were often seen. Worn over the right pocket are Vietnamese Special Forces (VNSF) jumpwings. Shown here are the more common Vietnamese pattern, but wings embroidered in US style were sometimes worn. VNSF jumpwings were awarded honorarily to USSF troopers, and US jumpwings were likewise awarded to VNSF personnel. Over his US jumpwings he wears the combat medic badge. All other team members were eligible for the combat infantryman's badge after serving at least 30 days as an advisor and being involved in at least two offensive ground actions. On his left pocket is worn the VNSF patch to signify his advisory rôle: A Teams assigned to Camp Strike Forces, B and C Teams, and Group Headquarters personnel all wore this patch. Those assigned to Mobile Strike Forces and reconnaissance projects did not. (USSF officers wore the Vietnamese equivalent of their rank between the second and third buttons on the front opening of the shirt.) This medic—commonly referred to as 'Bac Si', Vietnamese for 'doctor', by both the indigenous troops and fellow team members—is on a MEDCAP (medical, civic action programme) mission at a village near his camp. These areas were normally fairly secure and for this reason he is armed with only a .45cal. M1911A1 pistol in an M1916 holster. Another reason for the pistol is that it was regarded as a sign of authority by the Vietnamese and was often worn when dealing with them.

F1: Sergeant First Class, 3rd Mobile Strike Force, Detachment A-302, 5th SFGA; Vietnam, 1966
This NCO, assigned directly to a Mike Force Company, is wearing an early pattern of the tiger-stripes, which began to be issued in the early 1960s. The small 'cigarette' pocket on the trousers, and also found on some shirt sleeves, was in fact intended for field dressings. His jungle boots are the early version without the reinforcing straps at the ankles. He wears a red, white and blue scarf, popular with many Mike Force units. In some Mike Forces different coloured scarves—e.g. bright green—were presented as unit level awards to individuals. On his shoulder he wears the old Mike Force patch. It was banned from wear by non-SF higher headquarters, as the skull and crossbones did not fit the image desired for Free World forces; and it was felt that the meaning of 'M.F.' might be misinterpreted. . . . It was officially replaced in 1968 by a patch similar to the one worn by E2, but with a black parachute behind the tiger's head. He is armed with the older M16 rifle with the prong-type flash-hider (which caught on branches) and did not have a bolt assist assembly on the right side. On his M1956 LBE are M26 fragmentation and M18 coloured smoke grenades, the latter available in yellow, red, green, and violet.

F2: Specialist Five, 2nd Mobile Strike Force Command, Detachment B-20, 5th SFGA; Vietnam, 1969
This man characterises the enlargement and general upgrading of Mike Forces in 1968–69. He wears the newer style US size tiger-stripes which actually fitted Americans—who usually had to make do with 'large' Asian uniform sizes. On his pocket he wears the 2nd Mike Force patch; this was normally worn by the strikers, but some USSF also wore it. 2nd Mike Force USSF personnel had their own elaborate 'dragon' pocket patch, but these were not worn in the field. The standard helmet, with a Republic of Korea Army camouflage cover, is being worn due to the more conventional nature of their operations. His jungle boots have the 'Panama' soles, named for the area where they were developed; the cleated sole was designed to reduce

Members of the 1st SFGA on a Navy landing craft, 1969. A mix of full-colour and subdued insignia were often worn during the change-over period. (US Army)

mud build-up. The indigenous rucksack appeared in the early 1960s, and was modelled on the NVA version because of its practical design, ease of manufacture, and the fact that from a distance it would assist the wearer to appear as an NVA or VC. Most were made of a water repellent greyish green fabric, but olive green canvas ones were also made. His LBE is an M1937 Browning Automatic Rifle (BAR) belt. It has six pockets, each intended for two 20-round BAR magazines, but in this case four 20-round XM177E2/M16A1 magazines are carried. The belt was a popular, but somewhat scarce item. It did have the disadvantage that M1956 LBE items could not be attached to it; this trooper probably went to great lengths to scrounge an M1936 canteen carrier and M1942 first aid pouch. On his left hand M1956 suspender is attached an SDU-5/E strobe light (one of several models) in a nylon case; its beam can be seen from up to ten miles from an aircraft, and will not destroy night vision. They were generally equipped with a flash guard (to prevent detection from the ground) and a blue filter (so that the aircrew would not mistake it for a muzzle flash); an infrared filter was also available. His weapon is the XM177E2 sub-machine gun, a lightweight version of the M16A1 with a telescoping stock. Usually referred to as the CAR-15 (Colt Automatic Rifle), it was extensively used by Mike

51

An 8th SFGA mobile training team member instructs recruits of the El Salvadorian Army at its Sonbonate Recruit Training Center, September 1971. (US Army)

Force and reconnaissance project personnel. An M33 'baseball' fragmentation grenade, greatly improved over the old M26, is also carried.

F3: CIDG Striker, Plei Mrong Camp Strike Force; I Corps Tactical Zone, Vietnam, 1964

The spotted pattern camouflage uniform was used from the late 1950s until fully replaced by tiger-stripes in the mid-1960s; it proved to be rather ineffective, as it was not green enough for Vietnam's lush jungles, and its light colour was conspicuous. Olive green and black uniforms of a similar design were also worn by the early Strike Forces. The caps, too, were available in those colours as well as in tiger-striped pattern. His boots are the early olive green canvas, rubber soled 'Bata' pattern, often referred to as 'tennie' boots. The scarf is worn for 'friend-or-foe' identification; red ones were also worn as a deception measure, as many VC units wore them. His LBE is a World War II issue M1936 pistol belt with 15-round carbine magazine pouches (each holding two), M1936 canteen carrier, and the 'X' back M1945 suspenders. He is armed with an M1 carbine, capable of semi-automatic fire only. Other weapons issued to the early Strike Forces included M1903A3 bolt-action rifles, .30cal.;

M3A1 sub-machine guns, .45cal.; and even some former German World War II MP40 sub-machine guns, 9 mm.

G1: NCO, Reconnaissance Team Leader, Military Assistance Command Vietnam—Studies and Observation Group

This is a composite picture of a typical USSF Reconnaissance Team (RT) member. During the eight years that MACV-SOG existed, widely varying mission uniforms and combinations of equipment were employed: they changed with time, experience, the requirements of the mission, and other circumstances. The uniform pictured is jungle fatigues with black disruptive splotches spray-painted on. Although only used to a limited extent, it proved to be very effective in jungle shadows and at night. LBE items were similarly camouflaged. Olive green and camouflage jungle fatigues, jungle fatigues dyed all black, and the various patterns of tiger-stripes were also used. Olive green jungle fatigues were the most common, as the dark green colour had the appearance of an NVA uniform from a distance. Uniforms were sometimes soaked in insect repellent and air-dried before a mission. All manner of headgear was worn, including cut-down jungle hats and headbands made from issue triangular bandages, the latter being common, again due to their deceptive appearance. This man wears a black hat, as it was the 'VC colour of the day', a ploy used in their attempts to detect RTs. Jungle boots were the most common footwear, but efforts were sometimes made to leave deceptive footprints by wearing 'Ho Chi Minh' sandals, grinding the cleats off boot soles, wrapping boots with rags, or pulling thick socks over them. The US Army's Natick Laboratory even provided, on a test basis, a limited number of modified jungle boots with soles duplicating indigenous bare feet and sandals. M1938 canvas leggings were worn by some teams, as here, in an effort to keep out leeches. No insignia of any kind were worn, though most RTs did have their own unauthorised patches. They were sometimes sewn to the inside lining of USSF members' berets, while indigenous members wore them as pocket patches when in their Forward Operations Base.

All manner of LBE was also worn, although M1956 gear was the most common. STABO extraction harnesses were also used extensively (see Plate H1). The M1937 BAR belt was also popular due to its large capacity for magazines. Canteen carriers were often used to carry 30-round XM177E2/M16A1 magazines, as no standard pouch was issued for them until after the war. Another popular item were survival vests intended for aircrews, such as the SRU-21/P pictured here: Army olive green and Air Force sage green ones were both used. They had up to a dozen pockets, ideal for carrying the many required air-to-ground signal devices and survival items. A knife scabbard and pistol holster could also be attached to them.

A wide variety of weapons were also employed, including the XM177E2 sub-machine gun (by far the most common); M16A1 rifle; M79 grenade launcher; some Swedish-made M-45/b 9 mm sub-machine guns (often incorrectly called the Swedish 'K') in the early days; and in certain circumstances, enemy weapons such as the AK-47, or special purpose weapons such as silencers for pistols and rifles, and night vision sights (starlight scopes). Handguns of various models were also carried, with issue M1911A1 .45cal. and FN-Browning 'Hi-Power' 9 mm pistols (originally purchased by the CIA) the most common due to their availability. Various types of hand grenades were carried for the purpose of breaking contact with enemy forces; this man carries an M34 white phosphorus smoke grenade, which has both a fragmentation and an incendiary effect as well as an extensive smoke cloud. A few teams even carried a 60 mm M19 hand-held mortar for breaking contact. This trooper carries a privately owned Gerber Mk. II fighting knife; the various models of Randall combat knives were also popular.

G2: NCO, Assistant Reconnaissance Team Leader, Project Delta, Detachment B-52, 5th SFGA; Vietnam, 1964
Project Delta, like the other 'Greek-letter' reconnaissance projects, utilised various uniforms, equipment, and weapons throughout its six year existence. Tiger-stripes were the usual uniform for these projects. The cut-down-brim jungle hat was greatly favoured by Delta, but headbands made from triangular bandages were also popular, especially if the individual did not have to be concerned with concealing light coloured hair. LBE was the usual M1956 gear with a lot of canteens:

The commander and sergeant major of the 46th SF Co. receive a unit award from the Deputy Commander of the Royal Thai Army Special Warfare School at Lopburi, Thailand, 1972. The USSF wear the Army Tan uniform. (US Army)

water was a constant problem for the RTs, as the enemy often patrolled along streams to limit their use by the teams as well as to detect signs of their presence. Collapsible two-quart canteens were popular for this reason. A can of serum albumin is taped to the suspenders yoke: this is a blood volume expander used to restore and maintain the blood pressure of severely wounded until they could be evacuated. Issue gloves with the finger tips cut off were effective in protecting the hands from thorns and vines, but allowed unhampered use of weapons. A compass was carried in the chest pocket and secured by a cord around the neck. In his indigenous rucksack this man carries an AN/PRC-25 radio for contact with his patrol base, forward air control and extraction aircraft. Both USSF members of an RT carried such a radio, along with an AN/URC-10A emergency air-to-ground radio. Delta initially used M16 rifles, but were later equipped with the XM177E2 sub-machine gun. A cut-down 40 mm M79 grenade launcher was carried by some RTs as a break-contact weapon.

G3: CIDG Mountain Scout; Plei Yt Commando Training Center, I Corps Tactical Zone, Vietnam, 1963
The Plei Yt Commando Training Center was operated by Detachment A-751, US Army Special Forces, Vietnam. Black uniforms were normally issued to these troops, while olive green and spotted camouflage ones were the normal issue to Strike Force companies. Headgear varied greatly and included various colour and camouflage pattern

The 5th SFGA chaplain and his assistant at Ft Bragg, mid-1970s. The chaplain wears a Ranger tab and Jungle Expert patch on his OG 507 'wash-and-wear' fatigues. The assistant wears a 'candy stripe' cut from a full-flash, as manufactured ones were not then available. His fatigues are the cotton OG 107 model. (US Army)

jungle hats and caps, and brown berets. LBE was minimal and usually consisted of World War II gear. The M3A1 sub-machine gun, .45cal., commonly referred to as the 'grease gun', was standard issue for Strike Force Reconnaissance Platoons at this time; flash-hiders were almost universal issue.

H1: Staff Sergeant, Ranger Instructor, Detachment A-41, 46th SF Company; Thailand, 1972

Detachment A-41 (Ranger) was responsible for instructing the Royal Thai Army (RTA) Ranger School, a component of the RTA Special Warfare Center. All of the team's personnel were Ranger-qualified; many of the NCOs had been instructors in the US Army Ranger Department, and were directly reassigned to A-41. The team was additionally tasked with clandestine missions in Laos and Cambodia. Olive green jungle fatigues were the authorised uniform, but often, for instructor duties and while conducting operations with Thai Rangers, its members wore standard-issue black Thai Ranger fatigues. These were not merely dyed jungle fatigues, but Thai-made with black fabric. Worn with this uniform was a black beret with the 46th SF Company flash topped by a Ranger tab. A green beret was still the standard headgear with other uniforms. The Thai-made US badges and insignia were embroidered black on either an olive green or black backing and were

often intermixed. On his right shoulder this NCO wears an unauthorised combat patch (i.e. that of his former unit)—Deputy Chief, Joint US Military Assistance Group, which was the cover designation for US advisors inside Laos. The SF patch and Ranger tab would be on his left shoulder. On his right chest pocket he wears a badge denoting service with the Royal Palace Guards. Over the right pocket are Thai jumpwings. These insignia were only worn for instructor and training duties, and not on combat operations.

The LBE is made up of a combination of items. It includes a nylon Modernized Load Bearing Equipment (MLBE) utility belt with a quick-release buckle (which was not too popular, as it often came unfastened at the wrong times); Laotian issue M16 ammo pouches, originally made by the CIA as sterile equipment and subsequently adopted by the Laotian Army; and a STABO extraction harness in lieu of normal LBE suspenders. The MLBE system consisted of all nylon items and was basically an interim system introduced in 1967 prior to the adoption of the ALICE system.

The STABO extraction system was developed by SF instructors at the MACV Recondo School: STABO is the combined initials of the five NCOs who developed it. The system was intended to be an improved and safer replacement for the earlier McGuire, Hanson, and Palmer rigs, also developed by SF NCOs. The STABO harness is normally worn with the leg straps unfastened and rolled up, secured to the back of the utility belt. The system is intended to extract from one to four men from a site where a helicopter cannot land. The necessary number of 147 ft ropes are dropped in deployment bags to the ground party. They attach the web bridle to their harnesses, and the chopper lifts them out. They cannot be hoisted into the aircraft with this system, but are flown, suspended under the aircraft, to an area where a safe landing is possible. Here they are lowered to the ground, the helicopter sets down, and the personnel board it.

This soldier has a strobe light and the excellent Air Force survival knife attached to the STABO harness. The Thai ceremonial dagger was not just for show: it was recognised as a sign of authority by Thais, and was in fact issued to SF personnel involved in advisory duties. He is armed with an M16A1 rifle.

H2: 1st Lieutenant, Executive Officer, Detachment A-45, 46th SF Company; Thailand, 1972

Detachment A-45 (Special Missions), like A-42, was a team directly under the control of 46th Company Commander and used for special assignments such as Operation 'Freedom Runner'; these were operations conducted with the Cambodian SF. These two teams also conducted special reconnaissance missions in support of the RTA 2nd and 1st SF Groups respectively. Other teams directly under 46th Company Commander's control were: A-41 (Ranger), A-43 (SCUBA), and A-44 (HALO).

The lieutenant wears the standard RTA SF camouflage fatigues, which were popular among USSF personnel in the 46th Company. Over his right chest pocket he wears Cambodian jumpwings. On the left pocket flap is the 'Special Unit' tag worn by all organisations which supported the RTA Special Warfare Center. Another unauthorised combat patch is worn on his right shoulder: one of several designs worn by the Military Equipment Delivery Team, Cambodia (MEDTEC). These insignia were worn only while conducting advisory and training duties and not on active missions. The lieutenant's bar and infantry crossed rifles are worn horizontally and parallel with the lower edge of the collar, which was Thai practice, and one of the hazards of using local tailors. His LBE is the MLBE system, with the addition of a STABO harness. He is armed with an XM177E2 sub-machine gun. On the ground is a forest penetrator. This device is used on rescue hoist equipped helicopters. It has a weighted nose and folding blade seats that allow it to penetrate through interlaced tree branches. One to three men can be hoisted into the helicopter on the penetrator, which has safety straps that allow the individuals to be secured to the seat during hoisting.

H3: Surface-To-Air Recovery System

The Fulton Surface-To-Air Recovery (STAR) system was developed jointly in the early 1960s by the Army and Air Force under Project 'Sky Hook'. It provides a means of recovering personnel or equipment with long-range transport aircraft from areas that are out of range of helicopters. The Fulton system is fitted to some MC-130H *Combat Talon Blackbird* special mission aircraft operated by USAF Special Operations Squadrons, and was also fitted to some CV-2B *Caribou* aircraft of SFGA Aviation Companies. The STAR kit can be delivered to the recovery site by a cargo parachute dropped from the recovery aircraft itself or in a CTU-2/A aerial delivery container (see Plate C3) from a fighter aircraft. Kits can also be rigged in waterproof containers, with a rubber raft included, for water drops and recovery.

The STAR kit consists of two air-droppable bags containing a cartoon instruction board; an 8 ft diameter, 23 ft long balloon; one of two strengths of 500 ft long nylon lift lines intended for either one or two men, or 250 or 500 lbs of equipment/materials respectively; two helium bottles; an insulated nylon coverall suit with an internal harness; marker flags, for day use, and strobe lights for night use; and a remote control device to turn on the strobe lights (the aircraft also has a light-activation device, but it seldom works).

To accomplish pick-up a recovery zone of only 100 ft in diameter is required. Obstacles outside of this circle can be up to 50 ft in height. The individual to be recovered is suited up, attached to the lift line, and sits on the ground facing in the direction from which the aircraft will approach. The balloon is then inflated and released. The recovery aircraft approaches the balloon, into the wind, with its lift line yoke arms extended. It snags the line in a locking device on the nose, and the balloon's breakaway extension cords detach themselves. There are cable fendlines running from the base of the yoke arms to the wingtips to prevent the

A student A Team commander briefs team members during their Phase III unconventional warfare exercise in Uwharrie National Forest, North Carolina, late 1970s. The centre man is dressed to blend in with the 'guerrillas'. (US Army)

lift line from fouling the props in the event of a miss. The individual is lifted off the ground (rather slowly at first), and is towed behind the aircraft until the line becomes parallel to its belly. A cable with a hook, attached to a powered winch, is lowered to retrieve the lift line, and pulls it and the individual into the rear ramp door. Since this system's introduction in 1964 there have been over 200 live extractions with only one fatal lift line failure.

I1: Sergeant First Class, Task Force Ivory Coast; Son Tay Prison, North Vietnam, 1970

The raid on the Son Tay Prison on 21 November 1970 was probably one of the most expertly executed rescue missions in modern history; tragically, however, it proved a 'dry hole'. The 65 American prisoners of war being held there had been moved to other prisons shortly before the raid. The Army element of Task Force Ivory Coast were SF troopers selected from the 6th and 7th SFGAs and commanded by Col. Arthur 'Bull' Simons. They were inserted into the prison compound and surrounding area by Air Force HH-3 and HH-53 helicopters flown by Air Rescue and Recovery

Students of the SF Underwater Operations (SCUBA) Course, Key West, Florida. They have just completed their long-distance night qualification swim. (US Army)

Service crews. The soldier portrayed here is not a specific individual taking part in the raid, but rather a composite example.

A good deal of leeway was allowed in how the raiders configured their individual equipment. Their individual duty requirements also dictated this. Standard M1956 LBE was used as the basis for individual equipment. Canteen carriers were used to carry the XM177E2 30-round magazines, as no issue carriers had been adopted at this time. Taped to his left suspender strap is a miner's lamp and below it is a strobe light pouch. On the right suspender strap is an AN/PRT-4A radio transmitter (no receiver was carried, as he had only to report when he was in position). He has standard issue goggles with the addition of red press-on film to protect him from the air-dropped illumination flares. To protect his hands, but allow him to feel for locks and operate his weapons without the restrictions imposed by most gloves, he wears thin Air Force summer-weight flying gloves. Olive green jungle fatigues bearing rank insignia only were worn by all raiders. The XM177E2 sub-machine gun was carried by most of the 52 raiders. A commercial Armalite Singlepoint Nite Sight was fitted to each and reinforced with tape. Other armament carried by the force included M60 machine guns, M79 grenade launchers, M16A1 rifles, and 12-gauge riot shotguns. In addition, most carried an M1911A1 pistol and several hand grenades; most of these were Mk. III offensive grenades, commonly referred to as concussion grenades, due to their heavy blast effect with little fragmentation. Numerous items of survival and distress equipment were carried by all members. The patch is one that the raiders had made in Thailand before returning to the States; it was not worn on uniforms, but was a commemorative memento. The lettering stands for: 'Kept in Total Darkness/Fed Only Horse Shit'.

I2: NCO, Delta Force Operator; 'Desert One' Base, Iran, 1980

Delta Force's uniform during the ill-fated hostage rescue attempt was quite different from the usual standards of military dress. This was due to the unit's unique mission requirements and the need to blend into the population, at least from a distance. The 'uniform' consisted of an M1965 field jacket

(worn by many Iranian students and 'Revolutionary Guards'), dyed black; a dark coloured civilian shirt; blue jeans; wool navy watch cap; and some type of black boots. Issue combat boots were common, but 'Chippewa' climbing boots were favoured by many. On the jacket sleeve was a tape-covered American flag: the tape was to have been removed when the force reached the US Embassy in Tehran the following night. He is armed with a 9 mm West German-made HK5A2 sub-machine gun; telescoping-stock HK5A3s were also used. Other operators carried XM177E2 and M3A1 sub-machine guns, M16A1 rifles, and accurised M1911A1 pistols. The force was also armed with an M60 and an HK21 light machine gun, 7.62 mm, and a few M79 and M203 grenade launchers. LBE was not carried, as it would have made it too easy to spot an operator; extra magazines and evasion, escape and survival items were carried in the pockets and sewn into the field jacket.

I3: NCO, SCUBA Diver, 8th SFGA; Panama, 1972
SCUBA (Self Contained Underwater Breathing Apparatus) operations as conducted by Special Forces units are primarily intended for infiltration into enemy-held areas. Underwater reconnaissance, rescue, and recovery operations, as well as some offensive missions, are also conducted. The Special Warfare Center has conducted a SCUBA course for years at Key West, Florida. Groups maintain some A Teams that are fully SCUBA-qualified. Besides normal SCUBA operations, such techniques as surface scout swimming and para-SCUBA are also practised. Standard sport and commercial-type SCUBA equipment is used on most operations, but there is a very specialised piece of equipment available. This is the CCR-1000 closed-circuit rebreathing system, which re-cycles oxygen so that no exhaust bubbles can be seen on the surface. Other diving equipment includes the navy SCUBA buoyancy compensator (which can be used as a flotation vest, but its principal purpose is to allow the diver to achieve neutral buoyancy once he reaches his planned operating depth); weight belt; M3 combat knife; Mk. 13 smoke and

57

illumination signal (one end burns orange smoke for day use and the other is a red flare for night use); depth gauge; compass, and dive watch. Items that require to be individually fitted, such as mask, snorkel and fins, are purchased by the individuals from sport diving shops. He has just completed re-assembly of the M79 grenade launcher which he carried in the waterproof equipment container.

J1: Staff Sergeant, A Detachment Radio Operator, 10th SFGA; Ft Devens, Massachusetts, 1983

The Battle Dress Uniform (BDU) was first issued in 1982. Its design is based on the jungle fatigues, but several of the more practical design features were not included, thus detracting from its value as a field uniform. It is infrared-absorbent, which gives it some protection from certain night vision devices. The BDU's thick 50 per cent cotton/50 per cent nylon fabric also proved to be too heavy for year-round wear. This became readily apparent during the 1983 Grenada invasion, when an emergency issue of jungle fatigues was made to some units. The Army will reintroduce the design improvements as well as issue a lightweight tropical/summer version in 1985: these will be basically the old jungle fatigues with the addition of the woodland camouflage pattern. On this NCO's left pocket flap

An A Team of the 5th SFGA at the Gabriel Demonstration Area, mid-1970s. They are clothed in the camouflaged jungle fatigues. (US Army)

is a SCUBA diver badge. Above his right pocket he wears West German jumpwings, which are available in US style embroidery and colours.

His LBE consists of ALICE equipment to include M16A1 30-round magazine pouches. The rucksack is the large LC-1 ALICE model, on which is an M16A1 rifle. The radio is the newly issued AN/PRC-70 with an OA-8990/P Digital Message Device Group (DMDG). The DMDG is a micro-computerised message device that will burst-transmit a message, which has been typed into it, in a matter of seconds rather than the many minutes required for manual Morse Code, thus making it very difficult for enemy radio direction finders to locate the transmitter. The DMDG coupled with the almost unlimited range of the AN/PRC-70 makes an excellent combination for the unique communications requirements of SF. This equipment replaces the older AN/PRC-74B radio and AN/GRA-71 coder-burst group.

J2: Major, B Detachment Commander, 5th SFGA; Exercise 'Bright Star', Egypt, 1982

The desert camouflage version of the BDU was developed in the late 1960s, but shelved as there was no pressing requirement for it at the time. It was introduced in 1982 for issue to units operating in desert areas. Units slated for Army Central Command (formerly Rapid Deployment Force—RDF) are among those issued with it due to their

possible deployment to the Middle East. The uniform is of the same design and fabric as the BDUs. A wide-brimmed jungle-style hat of the same camouflage pattern is available, but a helmet cover is not; units usually fabricate some type of cover, using sand coloured cloth. A dark grey parka and overtrousers are also issued with this uniform for wear during the cold desert nights; they have a mesh-like dark green pattern printed on them, limiting the chance of detection by night vision devices.

This officer wears a Pathfinder badge below his master parachutist badge. He wears minimal ALICE equipment and is armed with an M1911A1 pistol; a lanyard is required during training exercises to prevent loss. The old M1923 cotton webbing pistol magazine pouch is still in use even though newer models have been issued.

J3: Sergeant Major, Staff NCO, 1st Special Operations Command; Ft Bragg, NC, 1984

The Army Green uniform was adopted in 1957 and has gone through a number of minor changes since. The grey-green shirt replaced the tan poplin model in 1976. The grey-green shirt, in conjunction with the Army Green trousers, may be worn without the coat. This uniform will replace the Army Khaki and Tan (tropical worsted) uniforms in 1985. Both long- and short-sleeve versions are available. 'Corcoran' jumpboots (a brand name that has become generic) are normal wear with service uniforms by all SF, Ranger, and other airborne units. Worn over the 1st Special Operations Command patch is the new SF qualification tab. The service stripes on the left sleeve each represent three years' service. The ribbons on the left chest are all individual awards while those on the right, in gold frames, are unit awards. Vietnamese SF jumpwings are worn above these.

K: Beret Flashes

Flashes are used to identify the various SF units and organisations. Abbreviations used are: Bn. = Battalion, Co. = Company, Det. = Detachment, Abn. = Airborne.

K1: Reserve and National Guard SF Units. This flash was worn by the Reserve's 2nd, 9th, 11th, 12th, 13th, 17th, and 24th SFGAs and 40th SF Det., and the National Guard's 16th, 19th, 20th, and 21st SFGAs, from 1961 until they were inactivated or adopted their own flash in the late 1960s or early 1970s.

K2: 1st SFGA. This was the original flash worn by the 1st from 1961 until the black border was added.

K3: 1st SFGA. To mourn the death of President Kennedy in 1963, 1st SFGA members added a black border to the flash with felt-tip markers. This outer black border was made official on 5 March 1964. Due to the difficulty of seeing it against the dark green beret, it was soon changed to an inner border; this was not made official until 5 November 1973. 'Candy stripes' normally retained the outer black border.

K4: 3rd SFGA. Approved in December 1963, this flash's colours represented the 1st, 5th, 7th, and SF Training Groups from which its personnel were drawn—and not the flags of Africa, as is sometimes reported. It was sometimes referred to as the 'trash' or 'Purina Dog Chow' flash.

K5: 5th SFGA. A solid black flash was originally envisioned in 1961, but a white border was added almost immediately for visibility against the beret. It was worn until K6 (below) was adopted.

K6: 5th SFGA. This flash was originally adopted by US Army Special Forces Vietnam (Provisional) in 1963. Its colours represented the 1st, 5th, and 7th SFGAs from which most of its elements were detached. The colours of the South Vietnamese flag are also depicted. Prior to the adoption of this flash the detachments wore those of their parent group. When the 5th SFGA deployed to Vietnam to assume the mission of SF Vietnam, the group requested that it be allowed to adopt this flash for tradition's sake, but also because it was felt that if SF personnel began wearing the black and white flash, it would be misinterpreted by the Vietnamese as the eradication of their national colours from the flash rather than as a simple change of insignia to conform with unit reassignment. This became the official 5th SFGA flash in late 1964 and was retained after it returned to the States.

K7: 6th SFGA. This flash was approved in 1963. Its colours represented the 5th, 7th, and SF Training Groups which provided personnel for this group.

K8: 7th SFGA. This flash was originally approved in 1961. Flashes of red naugahyde have been used.

K9: 8th SFGA. This flash was adopted in 1963, using the traditional SF colours.

SF crests: (Top, L to R) 1st SFGA, late 1950s—'arrows' are mid- and dark blue, background light green; 10th SFGA, late 1950s—background black and white; 77th SFGA, late 1950s—gold, black and white detail on teal blue.

(Centre) 1st Special Operations Command, right shoulder strap; 10th SFGA beret badge, 1955–62; 1st SOC, beret and left shoulder strap.

(Bottom) 1st Special Forces, since 1960; Walter Reed Army Institute of Research, worn by SF FEST—silver and maroon; Special Warfare Center and Institute for Military Assistance, since 1962—black and white background.

K10: 10th SFGA. This flash was approved in 1961.

K11: SF Det. (Abn.) Europe, and 1st Bn., 10th SFGA. This flash was originally approved for SF Det. Europe on 17 April 1969, utilising the German colours. In 1970 its wear was extended to Co. A, 10th SFGA which had remained in West Germany after the bulk of the unit returned to the States. In 1972 Co. A was redesignated 1st Bn., 10th SFGA. 39th SF Co. also wears this flash.

K12: 11th SFGA. This was approved on 8 November 1966 and replaced the SF Reserve flash.

K13: 12th SFGA. This was adopted on 11 January 1972, replacing the SF Reserve flash.

K14: 19th SFGA. This replaced the SF National Guard flash in the late 1960s. A lighter blue flash has been worn by this unit also. Naugahyde flashes are improvised and worn by some unit members, much to the ruin of bus seat covers in many cities!

K15: 20th SFGA. This flash was adopted on 27 June 1967. Another version was also worn, with a red border. Both were later replaced by K16 (below).

K16: 20th SFGA. This version was adopted on 8 May 1973.

L: Beret Flashes and Airborne Background Trimmings

L1: SF Training Units. The Special Forces Training Group (SFTG) flash was approved in April 1962.

SFTG was redesignated Institute for Military Assistance Student Battalion in 1972, and again redesignated Special Warfare Training Battalion in 1983, with both units retaining this flash. Its wear was extended to the SF School on 28 October 1981. White represented the unit's passive nature. Occasionally flashes made of white plastic or naugahyde were used.

L2: 22nd Aviation Det. (SF). This flash was authorised in 1962, but was short-lived, as the unit was inactivated the following year.

L3: 38th SF Det./Co. (Abn.). This flash was adopted in the mid-1960s by the 38th SF Det., Alaska National Guard which was redesignated a company in 1972, and inactivated in 1976. It employs the state colours. This flash is still worn by 207th Light Recon. Det. (Abn.).

L4: 46th SF Co. (Abn.). Approved for the 46th Co. on 30 May 1967, this flash was retained by that unit when it was redesignated 3rd Bn., 1st SFGA in March 1972. The flash's gold-yellow border and black background are the reverse of those of the 1st SFGA, with which the company had a loose association. The stripes represent the Thai colours.

Many of the unit members, especially in the early days, had been reassigned from the 1st SFGA and, at least initially, retained that flash.

L5: SF Det. (Abn.) Korea. This detachment's flash was adopted in the mid-1970s, and was based on the 1st SFGA's with the addition of stripes representing the Korean colours.

L6: SF Field Epidemiological Survey Team (Abn.). The FEST flash was adopted in 1966, and incorporates the colours of the Medical Department. Upon arrival in Vietnam FEST initially wore the 5th SFGA flash in the mistaken belief that this was required due to its attachment to that group. This was corrected and FEST was again permitted to

SF patches: (Top, L to R) Airborne Command, worn 1952–55— yellow lettering on black, white motifs on red; Special Forces, since 1955—yellow on teal blue, under yellow-lettered black Airborne tab, and yellow-lettered teal blue SF qualification tab dating from 1983; 1st Special Operations Command, since 1983—white horse, yellow lightning, green shield.

(Bottom) 3rd Army patch worn 1952–62 by Psychological Warfare Center and Special Warfare Center—white on blue, with red rim; Continental Army Command, worn by Special Warfare Center, 1962—white-on-blue tab, blue/white/red disc; Special Warfare Center and Institute for Military Assistance, since 1962—yellow-on-black tab, white lamp, yellow rim and arrows, red and yellow flames.

SF and CIDG patches: (Top, L to R) Mobile Strike Forces, 1965–67—white on black; 1st & 2nd Mobile Strike Forces, 1967–70—yellow on black tab, dark blue shield, black and white knife, red crossbow, yellow rim and lightnings; 3rd, 4th and 5th Mobile Strike Forces, 1967–70—yellow-on-black tab, dark blue shield with black rim, black and white knife, yellow lightnings; 2nd Mobile Strike Force Command, USSF only, 1968–70—basically white background, yellow and black details, with red flame and VN flag stripes.

(Bottom) The official Mobile Strike Forces patch, 1968–70, but note that other designs were retained—black and white 'chute and natural-coloured tiger on dark green shield; Camp Strike Forces, 1968–70—same colouring, no 'chute; Vietnamese SF (LLDB)—black shield, natural coloured tiger, other details white; Vietnamese Strategic Technical Directorate, the ARVN counterpart to MACV–SOG, 1967–75—red shield, light blue distant hills, natural coloured winged tiger, yellow lightning, other details black and white.

wear its flash from 27 June 1967.

L7: 1st SFGA Advisors. This was an unauthorised flash worn by some advisors from 1st SFGA in Vietnam from 1961 to 1963. It displays the 1st SFGA colours.

L8: US Army SF Vietnam (Provisional). This flash was worn unofficially by some SF Vietnam personnel in 1963 until what was to become the 5th SFGA flash was introduced. Its colours are based on the Vietnamese flag.

L9: White Star Mobile Training Teams. Another unauthorised flash worn by some members of the WSMTT in Laos in 1961. Most detachments of the WSMTT were provided by 7th SFGA, hence the red background. Unit flashes were not worn in-country due to political sensitivity.

L10: Individual Training Group/Forces Armées Nationales Khmer Training Command. This unauthorised flash was worn by this organisation in 1971–72. It depicts the Khmer temple of Angkor Wat. There were variations without the stars and with different colour borders.

L11: Special Warfare Center/Institute for Military Assistance. This flash was adopted in 1961, but not officially approved until 2 June 1965. It was also worn by the SF School until 1981. The black, grey, and white represent the three levels of propaganda.

L12: 1st Special Operations Command (Abn.). 1st SOCOM's flash was approved on 2 May 1983. Green represents SF, black Rangers, and white both psychological operations and civil affairs.

L13: Special Forces Background. It is interesting that this is universally considered the SF background and is worn by most units. However, it was originally approved for the 77th SFGA on 16 June 1954 and subsequently for the 7th. In the 1960s a number of new groups were formed primarily using cadres from the 7th. As these men transferred to the new units they brought with them the 7th SFGA's background. It was incorrectly assumed that it was intended for wear by all SF units, as it matched the colours of the SF shoulder patch worn by all units. The fact is that any SF unit may request authorisation for a background matching or similar to its flash.

L14: 10th SFGA Background. This background was approved on 12 December 1952. For a brief period it was worn by the 77th SFGA in the mistaken belief that it was intended for all SF units. A variation with a maroon, rather than a red border was worn by some individuals in the early days.

L15: SF Det. (Abn.), Europe and 1st Bn., 10th SFGA Background. This background was approved at the same time as the flash.

L16: 11th SFGA Background. This background was approved on 1 November 1967. The group wore the SF background prior to this.

L17: SF Field Epidemiological Survey Team (Abn.) Background. This background was approved at the same time as the flash.

L18: Special Warfare Center/Institute for Military Assistance Background. This background was adopted at the same time as the flash.

L19: 1st Special Operations Command (Abn.) Background. This background was approved at the same time as the flash.

L20: Army Security Agency Dets. Background. In 1961 the 400th, 401st, 402nd, and 403rd ASA Dets. were, for a brief period, authorised to wear their own background even though they wore their parent groups' flash. At the time the existence of these units was classified, and as a cover the background was officially listed for the 80th ASA Det. (Abn.) (Special Operations).

Notes sur les planches en couleur

A1: Tenue de service d'hiver—'rose et verte'—avec béret non officiel de fabrication allemande et insigne précoce 'Cheval de Troie'. **A2:** Uniforme d'été *khaki* en laine de qualité supérieure pour officiers et sous-officiers supérieurs. Notez les 'ailes' de parachutiste nationaliste chinois sur le côté droit de la poitrine—emplacement habituel des insignes auxquels le personnel des *Special Forces* pouvait avoir droit. **A3:** Gén. Yarborough fut le père des *SF* et du béret vert. L'écusson en tissu porté derrière l'insigne de béret était une habitude personnelle qui lui était propre. L'insigne d'épaule de la 3rd Army fut porté jusqu'en 1962 par le personnel du Special Warfare Centre.

B1: Parachutiste 'saut à haute altitude/ouverture du parachute à basse altitude' portant sa tenue personnelle de parachutiste avec insigne de club et bottes françaises. Le casque *MC-3* en cuir est porté avec masque à oxygène *MBU3P*. L'équipement de parachute *A/P28-3* possède un dais circulaire dirigeable. Notez la combinaison lance-grenades/fusil M203. **B2:** Parachute *MC-3* avec dais très manoeuvrable (voir arrière-plan) porté avec parachute de réserve circulaire normal. Sac *LC-1* attaché sous les jambes pour donner une plus grande liberté de mouvement dans une chute libre. L'uniforme camouflé de 1967 comporte les insignes d'épaule de son unité de combat précédente—*173rd Airborne Brigade*. **B3:** Pour sauts en parachute en forêt, une tenue de 'pénétration' est émise et un système de cordes d'alpinisme et de harnais est transporté pour la descente du parachutiste à travers les arbres. Notez le matériel de port d'armes sur la hanche gauche.

C1: Etudiant, portant un matériel démodé et un parachute *T-10*. Le sac est descendu avec une corde avant l'atterrissage. **C2:** Le 'même homme' mais portant l'équipement de 15 ans plus tard: uniforme de camouflage 'Woodland', parachute *MC1-1/B*, sac *ALICE LC-1*, fusil *M16A1* dans porte-fusil *M1951* et un mélange de ceinturons et de poches *ALICE*. **C3:** Le conteneur de matériel, portant 500 livres d'approvisionnements, peut être parachuté par un avion à réaction à une vitesse maximale de 680 km/h et à une altitude minimale de 91 mètres.

D1: Enseignant à ses élèves l'emploi de la mitraillette soviétique *PPSh-41*, il porte le béret de fabrication canadienne de l'époque et un uniforme *M1953*. **D2:** Utilisant une corde de rappel pour la descente en montagne, il porte une chemise en laine, des pantalons *M1953*, des bottes d'alpinisme 'Chippewa' qui sont un achat personnel et une casquette *M1951*. Il porte un fusil M14 et un matériel de démolition. **D3:** Tenue de camouflage de neige, portée par-dessus une *parka* verte et des pantalons d'hiver, avec toque d'hiver. Il tourne la manivelle d'une génératrice manuelle.

E1: Uniforme de camouflage 'à rayures de tigre', porté sans insignes et ceinturons

Farbtafeln

A1: Winteruniform—'rosa und grün'—mit inoffizieller deutscher Feldmütze und frühem Abzeichen des 'Trojanischen Pferdes'. **A2:** *Khaki*-Sommeruniform von besserer Wollqualität für Offiziere und höhere Unteroffiziere. Beachten Sie die nationalchinesischen 'Flügel' auf der rechten Brust—die übliche Stelle für ausländische Insignien, die Angehörige der *Special Forces* erringen konnten. **A3:** General Yarborough war der 'Vater' der *SF* sowie der grünen Feldmützen (Green Beret). Das getarnte Stück Stoff hinter dem Mützenabzeichen war keinesfalls gewöhnlich. Die Schulterinsignien der *3rd Army* waren bis 1962 im Gebrauch des *Special Warfare Centre* Personals.

B1: Fallschirmspringer mit dem Motto 'Grosse Höhe/Niedriges Öffnen'. Er trägt seine persönliche Fallschirmausrüstung mit Clubinsignien und französischen Stiefeln. Der *MC-3* Lederhelm wird mit einer *MBU3P* Sauerstoffmaske getragen. Zum *A/P28-3* Fallschirmzubehör gehört ein runder steuerbarer Schirm. Achten Sie auf die Kombination von M203 Gewehr/Granatenwerfer. **B2:** *MC-3* Fallschirm mit sehr manövrierbarem Schirm (siehe Hintergrund) und normalem runden Reservefallschirm. *LC-1* Rucksack, der zwecks Bewegungsfreiheit beim freien Fall hinter den Beinen befestigt ist. Die Tarnuniform aus dem Jahre 1967 trägt die Schulterinsignien seiner ehemaligen Kampfeinheit, der *173rd Airborne Brigade*. **B3:** Für den Absprung im Wald wurde ein 'Penetrationsanzug' sowie Kletterseile und Gurtwerke ausgegeben, damit die Springer sich von den Baumwipfeln abseilen konnten. Beachten Sie den Waffencontainer auf der linken Hüfte.

C1: Ein Student mit altmodischer Ausrüstung und einem *T-10* Fallschirm. Der Rucksack wird vor dem Landen an einem Seil abgelassen. **C2:** 'Derselbe Mann', allerdings mit einer Ausrüstung von 15 Jahren später: Waldtarnuniform, *MC1-1/B* Fallschirm, *LC-1 ALICE* Rucksack, *M16A1* Gewehr im *M1951* Container und eine Mischung aus *M1956* und *ALICE* Gürteln und Taschen. **C3:** Der Container mit dem 500 Pfund schweren Zubehör kann von einem Düsenjäger bei bis zu 542 mph aus nur 300 Fuss Höhe abgeworfen werden.

D1: Beschreibung einer sowjetischen *PPSh-41* Maschinenpistole vor der Klasse. Er trägt eine kanadische Feldmütze jener Zeit und eine *M1953* Uniform. **D2:** Beim 'Rappel' den Berg herunter trägt er ein Wollhemd, eine *M1953* Hose, selbst erworbene 'Chippewa' Kletterstiefel und eine *M1951* Mütze. Er trägt ausserdem ein M14 Gewehr und sein Sprengzubehör. **D3:** Schnee-Tarnuniform über grünem *Parka* und Winterhose und Wintermütze. Er kurbelt einen handbetriebenen Generator an.

E1: Tarnuniform mit Tigerstreifen ohne Insignien, sowie *M1956* Gürtel und Taschen. Der Schal weist auf die A-Kompanie, *5th SF Group*, hin. **E2:** Eine frühere Ausführung der Tigerstreifen, ein gestutzter Dschungelhut, 'Bata' Stiefel, *M1956*

et poches *M1956*. Le foulard indique la Compagnie A, 5e *SF Group*. **E2:** Version plus précoce des 'rayures de tigre', chapeau de jungle coupé; bottes '*Bata*'; équipement *M1956* et sac *ARVN*; et carabine *M2*, typique des troupes *CIDG*. Notez le foulard de la compagnie et les insignes de la compagnie sur la poitrine. **E3:** Le personnel des *SF* portait normalement un uniforme de jungle vert avec tous les insignes lorsqu'il n'était pas en mission. L'écusson des Forces Spéciales du Vietnam est porté sur la poche—Les *Camp Strike Forces* étaient 'officiellement' commandées par les *LLDB*.

F1: Sous-officier des *Mike Forces* portant les 'rayures de tigre' d'un modèle précoce et le foulard populaire chez les *Mike Forces*. L'insigne d'épaule fut interdit plus tard car on pensa qu'il 'faisait mauvaise impression' aux civils. **F2:** Les opérations ultérieures étaient plus importantes et plus conventionnelles, d'où la tenue de cet homme. Insigne de la *2nd Mike Force* sur l'épaule, mitraillette XM177, équipement personnel conçu à partir du ceinturon à cartouchière *M1937* pour *BAR*. **F3:** Uniforme à pois, porté des années 1950 jusqu'à l'introduction des 'rayures de tigre' vers 1965. Cet uniforme était trop visible et un uniforme uni vert ou noir lui était souvent préféré. Notez l'équipement personnel et l'arme remontant à la deuxième guerre mondiale.

G1: Il y avait beaucoup de variations dans la tenue et l'équipement de ces patrouilles de 'pénétration profonde'. Cet homme a sur ses pièces peintes en noir sur son uniforme vert, porte un chapeau *VC*, un gilet de survie d'aviateur aux nombreuses poches pour le transport de l'équipement, ainsi que des guêtres de la seconde guerre mondiale pour se protéger des sangsues. **G2:** Notez le bandeau de tête fait de bandages triangulaires, les nombreuses gourdes à eau, car l'ennemi surveillait les cours d'eau, les gants coupés, pour se protéger des épines et un lance-grenades *M79*, fournissant rapidement un feu puissant en cas de rencontres surprises. **G3:** Les uniformes noirs et les mitraillettes *M3A1* étaient typiques de ces unités de reconnaissance.

H1, H2: Divers insignes américains et des alliés étaient portés par ces hommes qui servaient avec les forces thaïlandaises. Le harnais *STABO* servait à soulever les hommes dans l'air lorsque le terrain ne permettait pas l'atterrissage de l'hélicoptère. C'était également la fonction du dispositif 'pénétrateur de forêt', illustré en avant-plan, qui avait trois sièges pliants. **H3:** Le système *STAR* comprenait une tenue avec harnais incorporé, un ballon, des bouteilles de gaz, etc. La ligne était lancée sur le ballon, attrapée par les bras sur le nez de l'hélicoptère, puis attrapée une fois de plus à partir de la porte de l'hélicoptère de façon à pouvoir monter le passager à bord.

I1: Un uniforme uni et un assortiment d'équipements choisi personnellement furent portés par les hommes lors du raid de Son Tay. Attachés au harnais, cet homme porte une radio AN/PRT-4A, une lampe puissante et une '*strobe light*' dans une poche. **I2:** Durant le raid de Téhéran, les hommes étaient principalement habillés en civils mais ils portaient un insigne national caché sur la manche, qui aurait été révélé s'ils avaient atteint l'Ambassade. **I3:** Un équipement de plongée en partie fourni par la Marine et en partie acheté personnellement est porté ici, avec le matériel de respiration CCR-1000, qui ne dégage pas de bulles. Le lance-grenades *M79* a été assemblé après avoir été transporté dans un conteneur étanche.

J1: L'uniforme *BDU* de 1982 sera bientôt remplacé car il n'est pas satisfaisant. L'équipement personnel est du type *ALICE*. Cet homme utilise une radio AN/PRC-70 avec dispositif de '*burst transmission*' micro-informatisé pour envoyer des messages à très haute vitesse. **J2:** Nouvel uniforme de camouflage de désert utilisé en exercice au Moyen Orient. **J3:** Uniforme de service vert 1957 de l'armée américaine, avec les derniers insignes d'unité, de qualification et d'ancienneté; certains insignes et certaines décorations du Vietnam sont aussi portés ici.

K, L: Les '*flashes*' des diverses unités, portées derrière l'insigne d'unité par les troupes et derrière les insignes de rang par les officiers. Les légendes en langue anglaises ne demandent pas d'explications dans la plupart des cas.

Ausrüstung und ein *ARVN* Rucksack; ausserdem ein für *CIDG* Truppen typischer *M2* Karabiner. Achten Sie auf den Kompanieschal und die Kompanie-Insignien auf der Brust. **E3:** Angehörige der SF trugen normalerweise eine grüne Dschungeluniform mit allen Insignien, falls sie nicht im Einsatz waren. Auf der Tasche ist das Abzeichen der vietnamesischen Spezialtruppe—die *Camp Strike Forces* unterstanden 'offiziell' dem Kommando der *LLDB*.

F1: Ein Unteroffizier der *Mike Force* mit älterer Tigerstreifen-Uniform und dem Schal, der in den *Mike Forces* populär war. Die Schulterinsignien wurden später verboten, weil sie angeblich Zivilisten den falschen Eindruck gaben. **F2:** Spätere Einsätze waren grösser und konventioneller—daher die Ausrüstung dieses Mannes. Insignien der *2nd Mike Force* auf der Schulter, XM177 Maschinenpistole, persönliches Zubehör, *M1937* Magazingürtel für sein *BAR*. **F3:** Die gepunktete Uniform, die in den 1950er Jahren bis zur Einführung der Tigerstreifen im Gebrauch war, war zu auffällig. Oft wurden einfarbige grüne oder schwarze Uniformen vorgezogen. Sehen Sie sich die Waffe und das persönliche Zubehör aus dem II. Weltkrieg an.

G1: Diese Spähpatrouillen hatten sehr verschiedene Uniformen und Ausrüstungen. Dieser Mann hat auf seiner Uniform schwarz aufgemalte Stellen und trägt eine *VC* Mütze sowie eine Lebensrettungsweste für Flieger mit vielen Taschen für seine Ausrüstung und Gamaschen aus dem II. Weltkrieg gegen Blutegel. **G2:** Achten Sie auf das Stirnband aus einer dreieckigen Binde und auf die vielen Wasserflaschen, da der Feind die Gewässer bewachte, abgeschnittene Handschuhe gegen Dornen und einen abgesägten *M79* Granatenwerfer, um schnell im Falle eines Überraschungsangriffs mächtig zurückzufeuern. **G3:** Schwarze Uniformen und *M3A1* Maschinenpistolen waren für diese Spähtrupps typisch.

H1, H2: Eine Reihe amerikanischer und alliierter Insignien, die diese Männer im Dienst der thailändischen Armee tragen. Sie trugen sowohl schwarze als auch grüne und thailändische Tarnuniformen. Das *STABO* Gurtwerk diente dazu, Soldaten von Stellen hochzuheben, wo Hubschrauber nicht landen konnten; demselben Zweck diente das Walddurchdringungsgerät im Vordergrund mit 3 Klappsitzen. **H3:** Zum *STAR* System gehörte ein Anzug mit eingebautem Gurtwerk, ein Ballon, Gasflaschen usw. Das Seil wurde am Ballon gelöst, von den Armen vorn am Flugzeug und dann von einem zweiten Seil von der Flugzeugtür aufgefangen und der baumelnde Passagier konnte hochgezogen werden.

I1: Einfache Uniform und persönlich ausgesuchte Zubehörmischung waren typisch für die Männer des Son Tay Angriffes. An seinem Gurtwerk trägt er ein *An/PRT-4A* Radio, eine starke Taschenlampe und ein '*Strobe Light*' in einer Tasche. **I2:** Beim Überfall auf Teheran trugen die Soldaten grösstenteils Zivilkleidung. Die schwarz gefärbte Kampfjacke hatte die verdeckten Nationalinsignien am Ärmel, die aufgedeckt worden wären, wenn die Truppe die Botschaft erreicht hätte. **I3:** Dieser Mann trägt teils Marineausrüstung und teils persönlich erworbene Taucherausrüstung mit dem CCR-1000 Sauerstoffgerät, dass keine Luftblasen abläst. Der *M79* Granatenwerfer wurde nach dem Transport in einem wasserdichten Container zusammengebaut.

J1: Die *BDU* Uniform von 1982 wird bald ersetzt, da sie nicht den Anforderungen entspricht. Das persönliche Zubehör ist eine Art *ALICE* Zubehör. Er bedient das *AN/PRC-70* Radio mit einem '*Burst Transmisstion*' Gerät mit Mikrocomputer, um mit sehr hoher Geschwindigkeit Nachrichten zu senden. **J2:** Die neue Wüstentarnuniform, die bei Übungen im Nahen Osten getragen wird. **J3:** Die grüne Uniform der amerikanischen Armee aus dem Jahre 1957 mit den neuesten Insignien der Einheit, der Errungenschaften und der Dienstzeit, sowie einigen vietnamesischen Insignien und Dekorationen.

K, L: Die Feldmützen-Stoffabzeichen der verschiedenen Einheiten hinter den Einheitsabzeichen der Truppen bzw. den Ranginsignien der Offiziere. Die Aufschriften in englischer Sprache bedürfen eigentlich keiner Erklärung.